Portraits

of a Few

of the People

I've Made Cry

Portraits of a Few
of the People
I've Made Cry

STORIES

Christine Sneed

UNIVERSITY OF MASSACHUSETTS PRESS

Amherst and Boston

This book is the winner of the 2009 Grace Paley Prize for Short Fiction. The
Association of Writers & Writing Programs, which sponsors the award, is a
national nonprofit organization dedicated to serving American letters, writers,
and programs of writing. Its headquarters are at George Mason University,
Fairfax, Virginia, and its website is www.awpwriter.org.

LC 2010027928
ISBN 978-1-55849-858-7

Designed by Kristina Kachele Design, llc
Set in Dante with Neutraface display
Printed and bound by Thomson-Shore, Inc.

Library of Congress Cataloging-in-Publication Data

Sneed, Christine, 1971–
Portraits of a few of the people I've made cry : stories / Christine Sneed.
    p. cm.
"This book is the winner of the 2009 Grace Paley Prize for Short Fiction"—Copyright p.
ISBN 978-1-55849-858-7 (cloth : alk. paper)
I. Title.
PS3619.N523P67 2010
813´.6—dc22
2010027928

British Library Cataloguing in Publication data are available.

FOR MELANIE BROWN

oldest and dearest

AND FOR MY PARENTS, TERRY AND SUSAN

Acknowledgments

I am grateful to so many people for their support and interest in my work, in particular the generous editors who have published several of these stories and bolstered my frequently flagging confidence: Heidi Pitlor at Houghton Mifflin, Stephen Donadio and Carolyn Kuebler at *New England Review*, Phong Nguyen and Kevin Prufer at *Pleaides*, Linda Swanson-Davies and Susan Burmeister-Brown at *Glimmer Train*, Brian Bedard at *South Dakota Review*, John Bullock and Jill Allyn Rosser at *New Ohio Review*, Gina Frangello, Lois Hauselman, and JoAnne Ruvoli at *Other Voices*. The very dear Tony Ellis. My teachers and friends at Indiana University, among them Maura Stanton, Alyce Miller, and Tony Ardizzone. John Buckvold and David Welch, writers and dreamers alike. Juan-Carlos Perez, Donald Evans, Randy Richardson, Noelle Neu, Jason Klein, Alison Umminger, Gregory Fraser, Mike Levine, Jonathan Taylor, Mona Oommen, Jennifer Barker, Lauren Klopack, Melanie Feerst, Ruth Hutchison, Dorthe Andersen, Denise Simons, Felice Dublon, and my colleagues at DePaul University. Lastly, thank you to Allan Gurganus and to the Associated Writers and Writing Programs. I am profoundly grateful to you all.

"Alex Rice Inc." appeared in *Pleiades* 30, no. 2 (2010), with the title
 "Student, Teacher."
"By the Way" appeared in *Other Voices* 21, no. 47 (Fall/Winter 2007).
"For Once in Your Life," appeared in *South Dakota Review,* Winter 2009.
"Interview with the Second Wife" appeared in *New England Review* 30,
 no. 4 (2009).
"Portraits of a Few of the People I've Made Cry" appeared in *New Ohio
 Review* 5 (Spring 2009).
"Quality of Life" appeared in *The Best American Short Stories 2008,* and was
 first published in *New England Review* 28, no. 2 (2007).
"Twelve + Twelve" is forthcoming from *Glimmer Train,* no. 76 (Fall 2010)
 and was the second-place winner in *Glimmer Train's* Summer 2008
 short fiction contest.

Contents

Quality of Life 3

Portraits of a Few of the People I've Made Cry 16

Twelve + Twelve 32

You're So Different 47

By the Way 64

Alex Rice Inc. 81

Interview with the Second Wife 101

For Once in Your Life 117

A Million Dollars 131

Walled City 147

Portraits

of a Few

of the People

I've Made Cry

Quality of Life

Mr. Fulger called when he wanted to see her and she obliged. For a while it was all very matter-of-fact, like a visit to the library, the reasons for going unequivocal. Regret rarely played a part. And there was little premeditation, as far as she could tell. Mr. Fulger, when not with her, resided on a plane that did not intersect her own, and after her initial period of infatuation had worn off, she had ceased to hope they might meet by chance. She had tried for a few weeks to find where he lived and worked, but he had remained unreachable, her attempts at tracing him fruitless, and soon she began to feel ridiculous to have spent the time searching for him—in their tremendous haystack of a city, he was smaller than a needle. In any case, she did not know what she had expected—certainly not a marriage proposal, nor more permanent terms for their involvement. It seemed to her that primarily she had wanted acknowledgment of his steadfast desire for her, however infrequently this desire was manifested. At times she saw him twice a week; others, twice a month. Even when she was dating another man—a man closer to her age who sought her out in earnest, publicly and otherwise—she answered Mr. Fulger's phone calls with a yes that triggered the naming of a meeting place, almost always a restaurant or hotel close to the center of the city, rarely the same one.

Mr. Fulger could not be his real name, because she had found only two in the phone book and neither, when she called them, had turned out to be him. One had died very recently; the dead man's brother had answered her call, informing her tonelessly that there would not be a funeral service but donations could be sent to a Vietnam veterans' charity. The other had spoken in a high-pitched voice that had possibly been female. "No," this person replied when she asked to speak with Mr. Fulger, adding that he was a tall man with salt and pepper hair. "I'm not the one you're looking for," replied the unpleasant voice. "Wrong number, Miss."

After a while it became evident that Mr. Fulger traveled frequently overseas, and at times he had gifts for her that were not extravagant, though it was clear they had been chosen with care. One evening he had given her a necklace with a heavy tiger's eye pendant; another night, a book from the Louvre. He knew that she could draw; she had once shown him a charcoal sketch of a mournful-looking elephant. She had meant to be funny, but he had admired the drawing and asked to see others. Aside from her sister and a few close friends, he was the first person who had shown more than a solicitous interest in her talent. He told her that he might want to buy some of her work, and when he saw how this surprised her, he suggested almost harshly that she take herself more seriously. She did not tell him that hers was a family long distrustful of artists, having been burdened with a legacy of schizophrenia on one side and depression on the other. Her accountant father and real-estate agent mother had objected strenuously to her choice to study graphic design in college, their tacit worry that if she met with failure, she would end up in an institution as her great-grandfather and his brother had, or else do herself in as had two poet-aunts years before, darkly inspired by Sylvia Plath and Anne Sexton. Whenever she heard these melodramatic stories told and retold by various family members over the years, Lyndsey remained dismissive, though in her private heart she wondered if theirs truly was a family more fragile than most.

She had met Mr. Fulger at a concert hall where she bartended during intermission, not long before she found a better job with a firm that designed theater programs. He had given her a tip much larger than the cost of his drink. He had also left his phone number, which had turned out to be an answering service. She had called him two weeks after meeting him, leaving her name and number, the concert hall's name as a reference. He had called back in less than three hours, inviting her to meet him for dinner that evening at an Italian restaurant on the top floor of a famously tall building.

"An old story," Mr. Fulger had said, sipping his wine. "The decrepit and shiftless enraptured by youthful beauty."

"You're hardly decrepit," she answered, barely suppressing a nervous laugh.

He smiled. "But perhaps I'm shiftless."

"I wouldn't know about that."

"And that is my good fortune."

"I know nothing about you at all." She felt a shiver climb her spine. His dark eyes unnerved her; he was grander, his manner more daunting, than the night they had met.

He nodded, not replying. She fidgeted with her napkin, not looking at him for several seconds. When she met his gaze again, his expression was mild, as if he were patiently listening to someone tell a dull joke.

Unable to match his silences during the hour and a half that they dined, she talked on and on about herself. He was possibly older than she had initially thought, somewhere in his late fifties instead of his late forties. She did not want to think that he might already have reached sixty. She was twenty-six. Her maternal grandfather was sixty-eight. Mr. Fulger seemed nothing like her grandfather, but she still did not want to imagine him her grandfather's peer.

She felt that in a way, however, she deserved what she got; if she were allowing herself to call strange men, the circumstances of their meeting would presumably be strange as well. This tendency to court real danger was new, something she would have to monitor closely.

The first night he did not suggest that they go to a hotel. He had instead taken her for a drink in a cavernous, smoky bar where a brass trio improvised discordant, rambling songs that would have impressed one of her former boyfriends, an unsuccessful pianist who violently detested his job as a receptionist at a popular radio station.

"Why do you live in this city?" Mr. Fulger asked.

She smiled, inexplicably embarrassed. "I went to college here. It's not a bad place to be."

"Will you stay forever?"

"Forever? I doubt it."

"Why stay at all if you know eventually you'll leave?"

"I wouldn't know where else to go right now."

"But at some point you'll meet someone who will."

Her face colored. "I don't know. Maybe."

"Of course, Lyndsey, of course." He smiled, swirling the red wine in his glass. "We often rely on others to make our most important decisions. There's no reason to be ashamed of this."

"But I don't think I've done that." She realized it might be a lie, though at that moment she did not want him to know it.

When they left the bar, he hailed two taxis, pressing money for her fare into her hand and brushing her cheek with his lips. She tried to refuse the money, but he turned abruptly away, disappearing into his own taxi. He had given her too much, fifty dollars for a twelve-dollar fare.

It would become his habit to give her money, and after a month and a half of seeing him, she would stop trying to return it. His money, indisputably, made her life easier. Also, the promise of his spontaneous reappearance enriched it, the phone call that arrived like a herald of what one day her life might be, though not necessarily with him: no more tiny apartments, nor the hopscotch from one debt payment to the next, nor the envy she often felt for those who wore impeccable clothes. In the end, the invincible protection of a powerful man's money and esteem, perhaps also his love. It would have been very easy for her to do much worse.

Mr. Fulger, whose first name was Reginald, though Lyndsey rarely used it, had a small chicken-pox scar below his right eye that she found fascinating in its allusion to his unknowable childhood. There was another scar on his chest, in the cleft between his pectorals. It looked as if he had been shot—the flesh puckered in a starlike pattern—but he had smiled with amusement when she had asked if a bullet might have made the scar. A bullet so close to his heart that hadn't killed him? No, no. He had burned himself many years ago, falling asleep with a cigarette in his hand, the pain of the fire against his bare chest causing a frenzied awakening. "I was out of my head, as I have rarely been in my life," he said. "It's never an ideal situation. A person who can avoid such situations is the one whom other people naturally flock to. And then, of course, all manner of deceit and handshakes follow."

Once she had said, "Why do you give me money? You don't have to."

He had not liked the question. "It's my desire to do so," was his curt reply.

Their affair seemed as if it would go on indefinitely, until one of them died or was otherwise spirited away. Never did he fail to take her to bed after the first night he had invited her to a hotel, asking first if she wanted a view of the park, which she had, its lights distantly reassuring, as if to say she was incapable of making terrible choices and suffering their consequences. When she closed her eyes and felt her body's warmth blend with his, there was the scent of cinnamon and then of smoke, a smell she could not detect on him at any other time.

From the start it was breathtaking—in part for her shame, in part for her astonishing pleasure. He was far from youthful, his body trim but slackening, his chest and stomach inspiring a twinge of sadness since it was clear that they had once been very firm and strong. How many women, she wanted to ask. How many have there been? It thrilled her to think that perhaps he had slept with a hundred or more. In sixty years, a hundred was not so many—if he had started young, that was only two or three a year. And not particularly unnatural since in all things except for sexual intimacy, variety was a virtue in human enterprise—experience, the sampling of the unknown, was a state of grace and laudable industry.

She told no one of her involvement with Mr. Fulger. For long weeks she wouldn't see him and when at last he called, she was sometimes tempted to refuse his invitation, to say that she had other plans, which at times she did. The one night she had done this, however, he had not called again for twenty-three days. She had known him for several months and was seeing someone else she liked more than usual, but they did not yet have an understanding. Like Mr. Fulger, the new lover called her when he wanted to; he did not appear to feel beholden to her in any way.

In her head a running tally of the amount of money he had given her sometimes arrived without warning. After eleven months: three thousand, two hundred and sixty-eight dollars. Not including dinners, gifts or hotel rooms. Because of him, she had been able to pay off one of her credit cards, and fly in her mother and sister for a long weekend, taking them to two plays. They had asked how she could afford it. A scratch-off lottery ticket, she had explained. Beginner's luck since she had never before spent money on such a foolish thing.

When Mr. Fulger called during their visit, she had made an excuse to her mother and sister. "A sick friend. I'll be gone for three hours, maybe four. I'm sorry about this."

Late that evening, on her way out of the hotel room, Mr. Fulger had given her an inordinately thick envelope. She saw in the cab that he had filled it with singles and five-dollar bills. She felt the chilly heat of acute embarrassment, as if she were checking a payphone for stray nickels, passersby laughing at her petty avarice.

And when she returned to her apartment with whisker burn, her sister noticed. "A sick friend," she said knowingly. "I wish I had a sick friend."

"I'd like you to move out of this city," said Mr. Fulger after a year of amorous meetings. "I'll make the arrangements. You could be closer to your family if you'd like."

She stared at him. "I don't want to move."

"I know someone who could give you a much better job if you allow me to make the plans for your relocation. I don't see what you have to lose." He regarded her. "Unless there's someone here you'd miss too much?"

"Most of my friends are here."

"You'd make new ones." He paused. "You've said yourself that eventually you'll move away. There's no reason it couldn't be next month."

She shook her head. "No thanks. Are you trying to get rid of me?"

"Of course not. I'd see you just as often."

"I don't want to move right now."

He sighed. "Think about it for a little while. Your salary would double."

She gazed at him in surprise. "What would I be doing?"

"The same thing you do here."

"I don't know if I should believe you."

"You can. Truthfully, you can. I'd arrange for a contract from your new employer."

"My god," she said, her stomach sickened.

He smiled. "It's not a bad suggestion, is it. Few would say you're making a foolish move."

"I haven't made up my mind yet."

"I'll check with you in the morning then."

No one else she knew lived like this. She was half enamored and half appalled by a man she knew nothing about, other than the intimacies of his body, his style of love-making, a few other superficial details. She knew his voice well enough that she recognized it the moment he spoke a syllable into the phone; she knew some of the foods he favored (salmon over beef tenderloin, quail over chicken). She had never seen him drive, did not know if he could. She thought it odd that he carried no keys. All that he removed from his pockets before taking off his tailored slacks were a billfold with only two credit cards; a money clip with several crisp bills; a few coins; a linen handkerchief, usually pale blue. His address was never on any of the items he carried; she had checked several times, risking this indecency while he used the bathroom. The only time she had ever seen him angry was on a night when a young thief had tried to steal her small beaded purse from the back of her chair in a quiet, exclusive restaurant. Mr. Fulger had risen from the table, motioned to the maitre-d', the thief then stopped at the door with Lyndsey's purse hidden under his overcoat.

"You might know the expression, 'If thy hand offends, cut it off,'" said Mr. Fulger, fuming at the craven, inappropriately handsome thief outside the restaurant while they waited with a security guard for the police.

She had wanted to leave, feeling the thief's fear and humiliation almost as her own, but Mr. Fulger had made her stay with him until the police arrived. "They'll need your testimony," he insisted, looking from her to the thief. "I'm sure this isn't his first offense. He knew what he was doing. But obviously so did I."

Certain words she did not allow herself to consider—concubine, whore, slut. Early on she had come to think of the money she took from him as a gift. If he had been her father, sending her money once a month because he worried about her well-being, few would have faulted her for keeping it. Mr. Fulger as well appeared to worry about her well-being. His money was meant to make her happy and specifically there could be nothing wrong with this. He insisted; he was forceful, persuasive, right about so many of the observations he made while in her company. She would have continued to see him if he stopped paying her. At least, she considered this to be true since she could not imagine not seeing him. The sex was satisfying, often thrilling. The money was simply something extra. Many would have said, once their moralizing had been proven specious, that she was very lucky.

The new job was far away, on the coast farthest from where she currently lived. Instead of theater programs, she would be designing print ads for feature films. Her parents would only be a three-hour drive if she agreed to accept Mr. Fulger's offer. The night of the offer she didn't sleep. She regarded the contents of her studio apartment, the new sofa, the sleek Chinese screen, the walnut hat stand that was purely ornamental. She sat in the window seat, looking down at the cars streaming toward and away from the city's center. She had grown to adore her small place, unsure if she could leave it so hastily, despite the promise of a doubled salary. She knew that Mr. Fulger had not lied to her; his offer, indisputably, was valid. But she did not know that she would accept it until he called her in the morning, at precisely eight o'clock. It seemed wrong to her, but she could not decide why. A terrifying thought arrived—perhaps this was the first stage of madness.

Though she also knew that always trying to be logical was equally mad. If a spectacular chance came along, it would be foolish not to take it.

"You should put in your notice today. The new office will expect you to be moved in and ready to start with them in four weeks."

She felt panic rise up, her heart stammering. "You said a month."

"Give or take a few days. Four weeks is hardly less than a month."

"I suppose you're right," she said, defeated. "But it's so soon."

"Maybe, but not unmanageable. You'll be fine."

After she hung up, she sat on her bed and sobbed. It was all so ridiculous. She had been handed an enviable new job and was now mourning her good fortune. She had previously thought herself pragmatic, prone to displays of cool appraisal, bracing practicality, sometimes at the expense of those who deserved better from her.

The man she was seeing still had not declared himself to her, but when she told him the following evening that she would be moving across the country, he said that he did not want her to go.

"Is there any way that you could stay a little longer, maybe a few more months?" he asked.

She shook her head, wanting to explain but unable to do it. He trusted her, even though they had never declared their feelings to each other.

"I could fly out there to visit, I suppose," he said.

"Of course," she said. "That'd be nice."

"You never told me that you were looking for another job."

"I wasn't," she said. "It came out of nowhere."

"Are you sure it's what you want?" he murmured.

"I think it is," she said, smiling wanly.

Her family was happy for her, pleased that she was moving closer to where she had grown up after so many years in a city they considered dangerous, and also prone to abominable weather for half of the year, if not more. The new job sounded interesting, and surely at some point she might even meet a few movie stars? (Even so, they did not want her to be seduced by these glamorous actors' reckless lifestyles—she should have a good time but keep her wits about her!)

Lyndsey did not know who Mr. Fulger knew at the firm that had hired her. She risked a few awkward inquiries shortly after she started but was rewarded with blank stares. No one had heard of anyone named Mr. Fulger. Was she sure it wasn't Fellsted? Or Fulstein? She tried again, using only his first name. No. No Reginald. Only a Ronald. A Gerald too.

Mr. Fulger kept his word; he began calling not long after she had settled in, taking her out to new restaurants and chic hotels that had been built into verdant mountainsides.

"We could go to my new place instead sometime," she said during their third meeting in the new city. "It's more spacious than my old apartment."

"I'm sure it is," he said. "But it's your refuge, not mine."

"I wouldn't mind sharing."

He shook his head. "I prefer hotels."

"Why?"

He gazed at her, his face more tired than usual. "The possibilities."

She was unhappy with his reply, with her new job, with her loneliness.

"Where is your wife?"

Surprise briefly transformed his features. "I've told you that I'm divorced."

She looked at him, doubtful.

"It's of no consequence, Lyndsey."

"So I'm the only one?"

He took a long time to reply. "In a way, yes."

"Why did you make me move?"

"I didn't make you do anything. You chose to move."

"You basically forced me."

He shook his head, his expression tolerant. "The position opened and I knew it'd be a good match for you. You couldn't disagree."

"I don't like it."

"Not yet."

"I want to go back."

He sighed. "You've been here for four weeks. Hardly more than a blink of an eye when measured against your entire life."

Her other lover soon flew out to see her, his delight with her new situation causing her to question her displeasure. "You've got it made," he said. "I'd move here tomorrow if I could find a set-up like this one."

"Maybe you could. I could ask around."

"We'll see," he said. "I'll do a little research first."

But after he left, she did not hear from him for several days, and he admitted when they spoke that he had not started looking for something closer to her. Mr. Fulger was also curiously silent. A month passed, then another. Perhaps he had seen her with her lover during his visit and had felt jealous, angered to find her enjoying herself with a much younger man. Countless times she had wondered if she had ever passed by a store or an apartment building where Mr. Fulger stood looking out at her. It had always seemed possible that he might spy on her or else hire someone to do it for him, but of course she had never caught him or noticed anyone following her.

She began to wake in the middle of the night, feeling keenly the absurdity of their relationship. It could not continue. When at last he called after ten weeks of silence, she told him that she wanted everything between them to stop.

"No," he said simply.

"Why not?" she said.

"Because this requires almost nothing of you. I've never been stingy, you'd have to agree."

"But I don't want to do it anymore. It's become too upsetting."

"You're being foolish," he said, naming a hotel, giving her an address. "Come out tonight and I know you'll feel better."

In their room, he had two dozen pink roses waiting for her. He spent time on her body, more than usual. She started to cry, her face buried in his shoulder.

"Do you want more money?" he asked, drawing away. "Would that make it easier?"

She shook her head, covering herself with the sheets. "I have more than enough now."

"I doubt that," he murmured.

"We have to stop this before I go crazy."

He sat up, his face hardened with displeasure. His thick, graying hair stood up on one side of his head, giving him a comical air in spite of the scowl. She wiped roughly at her wet cheeks, hoping her mascara hadn't run.

"Quality of life has greatly improved for you since we've met," he said.

"I don't know if I agree."

He regarded her. "Don't be melodramatic."

"Why can't I ever call you? Why did you wait two months to call me?"

"I was away on an extended business trip."

"Doing what?"

He hesitated. "I have never understood why people feel the need to know everything about each other. What would it change if I told you how I spend my time when I'm not with you?"

"I wouldn't feel so much like I'm sleeping with a stranger."

He shook his head. "It's clear that you have no trouble enjoying it."

"I'm going to say no the next time you call."

His expression was noncommittal. "We shall see."

"What do you do for a living?"

He sighed. "I sell clothing. I own several factories. Some in Asia, some in Eastern Europe. That's all."

"Couldn't I travel with you sometime?"

He gave her an unreadable look. "I don't think so, Lyndsey. That wouldn't work very well. You wouldn't enjoy yourself anyway. I'm always in meetings."

After a time, things again became routine, her former life and her regret at its loss receding—she went to work, she had dinner on occasion with a few people who were now her friends, she saw other friends from high school who lived in the city or occasionally visited it. Her lover on the other coast began to see someone else. She met a man who worked for a movie studio for whom she designed posters. Mr. Fulger called every two or three weeks, their lovemaking predictably, perversely satisfying. After ten months, the man from the movie studio asked her to marry him. She said yes and told Mr. Fulger that she would have to stop seeing him because of her engagement.

Again he said no.

She felt more desperate than she ever had with him. "It has to stop," she said. "I could pay you back everything you've given me."

"No. I'm not interested in a refund."

"I want to marry this man."

"Fine. I won't stop you, but you and I will still be seeing each other after your marriage. That's all I require."

"Please find someone else."

He shook his head. "You suit me perfectly. It wouldn't be as pleasurable with someone else."

She left him that night thinking that she would have to move, request an unlisted phone number, dye her hair, change jobs, attempt everything to get away from him. She would ask her fiancé if they could move far away and find new jobs; she would say she was tired of the traffic, the unhealthy air. They would do better to move up the coast, maybe work from home if possible.

But when she began to explain to him why she wanted to make these changes, her fiancé suspected the story wasn't complete and connived the truth from her. When he learned that she had continued to sleep with Mr. Fulger during their courtship, he broke off their engagement, explaining that it might be old-fashioned in their permissive times to be upset about such a thing, but he couldn't help his innate squeamishness when it came to infidelity. He marveled as well over her ability to be so calmly deceitful during their courtship. Had she loved him at all?

"He is simply one man among the many thousands more you'll meet," said Mr. Fulger upon learning of the broken engagement. "And I won't live forever. Or perhaps the next man you fall for won't mind me so much."

She made plans to leave the city, to move north to another state. Nothing else seemed possible—this, she recognized dimly, was hysteria. When the contents of her apartment were packed in boxes and ready to go on the moving truck, profound despair seized her. The moving men were sent away. She tossed one box from her second story window, narrowly missing a woman who walked by with a bag of groceries. "I should call the police," yelled the woman, staring up at Lyndsey from the sidewalk in fear and amazement, half of her groceries now spilled on the ground next to the ruined box of cooking pots.

"It was an accident," cried Lyndsey, trembling with horror. "I'm so sorry."

"You could have killed me," yelled the woman, angrier now. "What's your fucking problem?"

He did not understand why she remained so unhappy. She was not poor, or dying prematurely from some vicious illness, or imprisoned on wrongful charges, or grievously disabled, or the wife of an abusive husband in a place where religion made divorce impossible. Why was she wasting time feeling so sorry for herself? She had so much freedom, was accountable to him for so little, only a few hours a month, and it wasn't like he did anything but spoil her.

He had a point, of course. His logic, though it troubled her more than she could say, remained unassailable. She would not be released, even if she threatened to harm one or both of them, even if what he did to her became rape. What was so terrible about her situation, he wanted to know. She remained young and beautiful; she had a good job, a nice home, friends, a loving family. Obviously there were much worse things to lament if she would spend a moment or two considering the range of horrors just outside her usual frame of reference. She could of course be happy again. In the frankest analysis, it would remain, as always, her choice.

Portraits of a Few
of the People
I've Made Cry

Antonio Martedi, a painter and sculptor who had sold what he sometimes boasted were his least interesting works to American museums, told his granddaughter, April Walsh, on what turned out to be the day before his death, that he had not lived in fear of mediocrity so much as the disdain of beautiful women. He had made art because he wanted to be loved, preferably by many beautiful women in a slow but uninterrupted progression, women who would remember him fondly after their affair had ended and keep whatever sketches or canvases he had given them in an honored place in their homes. "But if after a while they sold my work for a good price to someone who knew how to appreciate it, I wouldn't have held it against them. The money would be another way for me to keep my place in their hot little hearts." This was the first time April had heard any of this, and she had no idea what had prompted it. Her grandfather had a reserve of stories that he repeated with depressing regularity for a man widely known for his flamboyance. She assumed that she had heard all he was willing to tell by the time she had graduated from film school and was failing to sell her scripts or to get hired as the production assistant's own scorned assistant.

The same afternoon that he made this unexpected disclosure, he gave her three of his old sketchbooks and ordered her not to tell anyone that she had them because then she would be tempted to sell them and this would greatly displease him. "Unlike the presents to my old girlfriends, if I wanted someone other than you to have these notebooks, I would have sold them myself a long time ago or donated them to some art school library."

Each sketchbook was a black cloth-bound diary, the pages unlined. One notebook held only ink and charcoal sketches of both men and women, mostly nudes. Another held small studies in pastels of notable buildings in Chicago, Philadelphia and San Francisco, all cities where her grandfather had taught as an artist-in-residence. The third held numerous sketches of household objects and women's faces, and a series of Matisse-like cut-outs of trees, skyscrapers, and the female figure that were like nothing she had ever seen him create on a larger scale. She imagined that she could have sold each notebook for thousands of dollars. But she would never do it.

It was the following afternoon at a quarter past one during a light snowfall that Martedi skied into a tree on a mountain in Breckenridge and broke his neck. April was with her mother on a different slope and they didn't hear about his death until two hours later. Hearing the news from a gray-faced doctor and a terrified ski-lodge official, she thought immediately of the sketchbooks he had just given to her and wondered what had prompted him to give them away. She knew that he hadn't been suicidal, and witnesses' accounts all concurred: he had hit a patch of ice, lost his poles, and slid at high velocity into a small cluster of pines.

The obituaries that ran in the *New York Times,* the *Los Angeles Times,* and *The Guardian* all mentioned his paintings, the early conceptual and the late-period figurative pieces, some of which hung in the Art Institutes of Chicago and Boston, MoMA and the Tate Modern, and his public sculptures, one of which was a controversial bullfrog-like structure that had once been considered, apparently without irony, a good candidate for installation in the spot where the Reichstag used to stand, but the frog ended up a feature of Manchester, England's urban renewal project. Also mentioned were his liaisons with politicians' daughters, TV actresses, lingerie models, former nuns, and cosmetic-company heiresses. *The Guardian's* obituarist wrote: "In several of his works, Martedi immortalized the dip of a woman's waist. He considered it one of two divine curves that validated God's existence. The breasts, of course, are the other divine curve. He considered the derrière a close third, by the way." The *L.A. Times'* obituarist likewise wrote: "He worried that American men would never be capable of adequately appreciating the beauty of American women, and for the last fifteen years of his life, he sporadically toured the country and gave free lectures and figure-drawing lessons to men of all ages and social classes. He hoped that a man's ability to lovingly capture the curve of a lover's hip or cheek with a charcoal pencil would save couples from chronic unhappiness."

At the time of his death, he was seventy-one and his girlfriend was a forty-six-year-old Norwegian-born sculptor named Lidia Bjur who lived in a Lower East Side walk-up that Martedi had owned and also lived in, bestowing a floor each to Lidia and one other tenant, an octogenarian widower who had agreed to sell Martedi the building for much less than it was worth if he be allowed to stay for as long as he wanted to. It was Lidia, a sexy and self-professed troublemaker, who introduced April to Barrett Hayes a few weeks after her grandfather had been cremated, his ashes flown to Rome and surreptitiously scattered by April, her mother, and Lidia on the Spanish steps just after midnight, as his will had made clear they must be.

According to Lidia, Barrett was a handsome misfortune—a long-lashed, floppy-haired painter in his late twenties who had sold several of his canvases at a respectable gallery in Chelsea a year earlier but lasting recognition had continued, most unfairly, he was convinced, to elude him. Lidia warned April that he was ambitious and restless and might be interested in her—no insult intended—solely because he hoped to claim some part, no matter how doubtful, of her grandfather's genius. April wasn't ugly or crass or untalented, but a lot of the women Barrett knew had as much visibly on offer as she did, as Lidia sternly made clear. It would be best not to get too attached to him—she should expect nothing complicated, and try not to get into anything with him likely to leave a mark. Sex if she wanted, yes of course, but she was not to let him get to her heart. Lidia would not say whether or not she had slept with him, so April assumed that she had.

As both women instantly recognized, Lidia had offered her what she knew would be a terrific opportunity to court disaster, yet another in the ever-lengthening line of her so far shockingly disappointing adulthood. But how often were these terrible opportunities as attractive as Barrett Hayes with his smoky voice and dusty, oilcloth-tinged scent? Not to mention his pretty lips, serious eyebrows, and his paintings of urban decay and feral animals in futuristic junkyards which April recognized as good if not great. This assessment, however, she knew to keep to herself.

Barrett liked to be called Barrett and he told her this with an ironic smile while holding her hand for a very long time after Lidia introduced him. He was a man who really, really liked to touch soft things and he told her this too. They were introduced at the memorial bacchanal organized in honor of Antonio's appetite for beauty and questionable behavior. Barrett stayed within whispering distance for most of the party, bringing April glasses of murky red wine, making her blush and feel idiotic, yanking off her clothes with his blue-gray eyes that she supposed had seen more naked women than she would ever want to hear about. At one point he said something jawdroppingly insincere that forced her to admit she would never underestimate her ability to abase herself: his words made her want to have sex with him immediately. "You're the type of woman I bet I could fall in love with," he murmured, holding her arm just above the elbow, apparently one of his many favorite soft places.

The "I bet" made her nervous because it implied the opposite—of course he wasn't sure. Not at all. Here was a boy in a man's body, a clever disguise that in her experience most good-looking boys had figured out how to use. But maybe she was being too cynical, maybe he was sure?

Yet there was no doubt, even in her wine-fuzzed mind, that he could not be trusted. "I bet not," she said, her voice too loud from the four glasses she had soaked down in the past hour and a half. "You don't know me at all."

"I know everything I need to know."

She snorted. "Stop lying to me."

He smiled. "I don't lie. Ever. And let me tell you a secret, April Walsh." He paused, and in that long second, she saw him in front of his bathroom mirror, testing the effect of these whoppers. She knew that he did it. He absolutely did. "Most people hate that I don't lie. Because the crazy truth is, lies are the only things saving us from extinction."

Go right through the door and never, ever talk to him again. *Ever.* This was the strident voice that she heard and promptly ignored. It almost always spoke up right before she was about to plunge into something fatally stupid, its timing ruthless. She and Barrett were standing next to a glowering portrait of a female acrobat that her grandfather had begun five years earlier and left unfinished. The acrobat lay flat on her back on a net, presumably having just fallen from the trapeze. This acrobat-model was at the party, her long black hair in the same fierce bun she had worn in the portrait. April had caught herself staring at the woman's long arms and legs; they were bare and enviably firm, shown off in the same purple leotard she had worn in the painting. Her name was Pony but April didn't believe it. Barrett, however, did, and she resented him for this.

They went to his apartment at one in the morning, not hers because she was staying with Lidia. Her apartment was in godforsaken Rancho Cucamonga, California, with all six and a half of her unsold screenplays and her unhappily divorced roommate. Lidia knew what they were up to and April didn't bother to pretend. Lidia gave her an unreadable look and said, "You can ring the bell downstairs at any hour. I'll answer it."

One thing became unexpectedly clear as soon as they were naked—Barrett had the roundest, firmest buttocks she had ever gotten her hands on. They were from bike-riding, he told her, obviously proud. For five years he had paid his rent by working as a bike messenger, and the muscular ass had stayed long after he had quit the job. "Who can reasonably accuse the working man of not being beautiful?" he asked with a grin, his hands smoothing her sides and long, tired legs, something no boy had ever done before with such tenderness.

"You're totally ridiculous," she managed to say, trying not to whimper as his hands and mouth had made their slow trek south.

He was much better than she had expected. Sadly, he was very close to phenomenal.

Despite the terrific chaos that had overtaken her body when he parted her legs and made his big move, her mind dimly recognized that his expertise at such a delicate, necessary task could be disastrous for her. For a fevered second, she had a picture in her head of the lunatic in *Fitzcarraldo,* a man obsessed with carrying a boat up a mountain.

When they finally stopped, he let her fall into an exhausted, dreamless sleep in the middle of his bed. The clock said 11:11 when she woke the next day with stiff inner thighs, chapped lips and whisker burn. It had been several months since she had slept with anyone but herself. The first thing he said while she was self-consciously scrubbing at the mascara flakes she suspected were lodged beneath her eyes was, "I don't like many people. Maybe eight or nine. Lidia is one of them. I trust her."

"That's nice of you, but I don't," April croaked, her voice stuck in the middle of her throat.

"That's because you're jealous of her."

She looked at him, taken aback. "No, I'm not."

He smiled, several strands of his floppy hair stuck to the corner of his mouth. She stopped herself from reaching up to brush them away. He would have thought it too intimate, despite where this same mouth had spent half the night. "We should all be jealous of someone," he murmured. "Jealousy is at the root of most desires."

"Please stop with the dimestore wisdom. It's way too early for me."

"It's almost noon, Mademoiselle."

"Noon isn't early if you stay up until four-thirty." He had worked her over for close to three hours. Only four other men in her life had tried to do what he had done to her. One had succeeded, the others had merely thought they had. Despite her suspicions about what he could do to her in the future, she felt grateful for all that he had done last night.

"I'm surprised you noticed. You fell asleep faster than anyone I've ever seen. You shut your eyes and it was like turning off a lamp. Out you went."

"My only talent."

He studied her. "You try to be so brittle and sarcastic but I know that's not really who you are."

She shook her head. "No, I'm soft in the middle like most sluts." The lunatic with the boat flashed through her mind again. She had a headache, a parched mouth and needed to pee but was afraid that if she got out of bed, she would never be welcomed back.

"I don't think you're a slut. I'm the slut," he said.

She gave him a wry look but said nothing. His hair stood out like a lady's fan behind his head—a peacock, she thought. It was an image she knew she would poach for the screenplay she had been trying for seven months to finish. Everything that had happened with him she would poach. He would love it if he ever found out, if she ever sold the work and became someone other than the renowned, lecherous, brilliant Martedi's granddaughter and stopped living with a very sad twenty-seven-year-old who kissed pictures of her unfaithful ex-husband and sobbed whenever she heard "The Girl from Ipanema." She forced herself out of bed and went down the hall to the bathroom where she looked in the mirror while peeing and decided her face was not that much of a disaster.

Several bars of fancy soap sat in a neat pile next to the sink—lavender, pear, almond-honey, magnolia, rose. Probably not a good sign, she thought. It also seemed that despite, or perhaps because of, Lidia's warning, she might be falling flat on her face for Barrett Hayes. It had happened to her before in a matter of hours. Like death and other natural disasters, when it was your time, it was your time. God, she already sounded like him. She frowned at the mirror now, staring at her tired face. She had no idea how much he liked her or liked looking at her, despite his asinine, wine-drenched avowals at the party. It seemed a safe bet that she was not one of his exalted eight or nine.

In ten minutes, she had dressed herself and left his basement apartment with its cloying smells of rancid cooking oil, varnish and dust. He had offered to get them bagels but she had shaken her head, convinced that her quick departure would seem like an escape to him; optimally, it would force him to feel insecure and question her feelings. She did not want to leave at all, but she knew that the fuck-and-run tack could work just as well when the female in the pair tried it. But he did not protest her refusal to stay for breakfast; he only gave her a quizzical look and said, "Okay, my sweet, suit yourself."

Four days passed before he called her, which was only two days before she was due to return to California. During his infuriating silence, Lidia was unfailingly gentle, putting fresh flowers in her room, telling her that she must be patient with the current circumstances of her professional life and keep writing—at all costs, keep writing.

One afternoon when April felt angrily heartsick and plagued by four o'clock malaise, Lidia grasped her arm and said that though Barrett was sexy, he was still a child and there was no mortal way around this. "If not him," she said. "Then someone else. You probably don't want to think about it, but it's true. I never thought I'd recover from my ex-husband, but I was wrong."

"I don't really like him. I hardly know him."

Lidia wasn't impressed. "You don't have to. That's the problem."

The two women ate breakfast together each morning, usually not before eleven, both of them preferring to stay up very late reading or working alone in their rooms. After yogurt and coffee, they would climb two flights of stairs and wade into the morass of Antonio's studio to tidy and sort. April's mother Beatrice, who was the executor of her father's estate, had already spent two weeks working through the stacks of canvases and sketches and half-finished sculptures, some of the figurative sculptures in costly Italian marble, some made of wood or sandstone or the rough media of burlap and tar paper. The gallery owner whom Antonio had worked with exclusively for the last twenty-three years had taken whatever Beatrice would allow, and the remainder had been left where it lay, for her and Lidia and April to confront when they found the energy to. Beatrice had left the day of the bacchanal, having bought tickets for a trip to Prague with April's stepfather months before Antonio had died. She had told Lidia and April to do what they wanted to do with the studio, but not to sell or throw anything away.

Her grandfather, unlike many other artists, had not been a packrat. But fifty-three years of art-making had resulted in a mountain of finished work along with colorful detritus and discards—five of them small, intricate paintings of women's morose faces that she had seen the preliminary sketches of in one of the notebooks he had given to her. The women were part of a series he had titled *A Few of the People I've Made Cry*, the other four portraits in the series having been sold several years earlier. April knew he could have sold these other five instantly if he hadn't thought them slapdash and immature. They weren't, but he could not be convinced otherwise once he had made up his mind. Nevertheless, his habit had been to paint over canvases that he considered outright failures.

When Barrett finally called her, offering no excuse for the four-day silence other than many hours spent in his studio, he asked if he could come over to look at her grandfather's studio before taking her out for dinner. "Yes," she said. "But no stealing."

"We'll have to see about that," he said mildly.

Despite being three rooms removed from the phone, Lidia knew who had called before April had said a word. "Make him pay the check. He needs to earn whatever you offer him." April wasn't sure if Lidia smirked as she said this. "It's none of your business," April wanted to growl. Instead she said, "I always do."

"Good," said Lidia but it was clear that she did not believe a word. She disappeared into the back room of the apartment where she kept a black-and-white TV and a fossil-grade CD player, vintage 1987. This was the same room where Martedi had often slept with her, Lidia had casually revealed on the night of the bacchanal; April rarely visited, the site of her grandfather's final old-man acts of virility flustering and a little obscene, in part because she thought Lidia beautiful but her grandfather not at all.

Barrett arrived with a small bunch of daisies and two fragrant, perfect white lilies. The lilies were for her, the daisies for Lidia. For a boy-man, she had to admit that he was unusually thoughtful. He kissed her cheek and gave her a naked look that made her feel sweaty, but he did not want to talk when a few moments later they stood together in her grandfather's studio. "I'm sorry, but it's a temple," he said softly. "It's the kind of place where the secrets of the universe reside."

She almost rolled her eyes but could see that he actually meant it.

"I know you think that sounds corny, but if they're not in art, then they're nowhere."

"Maybe," she said, unconvinced. "I guess I've heard that before."

"It's all right to hear it again because it's true."

The studio smelled inexplicably of black pepper, also of turpentine and burnt coffee. The room was narrow but long, with four tall windows, each dusty and with a few cracked panes that her grandfather had ignored for years, saying that if an art thief wanted to climb the side of the building and steal his work, he'd take it as a compliment. He had had an unswerving faith in his ability to make more.

Barrett went over to the unfinished painting of Pony, the acrobat. April's mother hadn't yet given it her father's art dealer because she wanted to touch it up before releasing it. Beatrice painted well but didn't often do it; she was a cellist by trade, her talents, like her father's, eclipsing most of her peers. April had spent much of her adolescence waiting for her own great talent to manifest itself, screenwriting something she had started at sixteen with arrogant expectations but had quickly found herself humbled by, especially in the inexorable way that the story and the characters, around page twenty or thirty, veered cruelly away from her. Some of these early scenes she had rewritten as many as thirty-four times.

Barrett studied *Highwire* for a long minute while she grew restless and jealous, wondering if he had slept with Pony during the four days she hadn't heard from him. She wondered if he had slept with everyone she had caught him glancing at during the night of the bacchanal. This has to stop! she thought wildly. I might as well be gouging myself with a rusty nail for all of the good it's doing me.

She knew that she might end up begging him for something he wouldn't want to give if she weren't returning to California in two days. She was twenty-five and in no danger of becoming a self-possessed woman. She also realized that in the past week she had probably become infatuated with Lidia, who aside from being beautiful was calm and talented enough to have had the same gallery representing her work for the past nine years. She didn't want to have sex with Lidia but she wished she could really know her, maybe hold her hand once in a while, be adored just as much in return.

When Barrett had stopped ogling *Highwire,* he spent several more minutes looking at the discards, marveling over her grandfather's expert brushstrokes, his stunning instinct for color and depth and light. When he finally looked again at April, he saw that she hadn't shared in his euphoria. "You're brooding about something," he said. "I would bet a hundred bucks that that's your natural state."

She regarded him. "No, not at all. But I do sometimes feel a little depressed when I come to New York. Everything's so dense here. With all the tall buildings, you have to fight for sunlight. It really starts to wear on me after a few days."

"This is the greatest vertical city on earth. We're living right in the middle of a myth," he said happily. "Where you live, it's all horizontal and embryonic."

"No," she said, shaking her head. "There are myths out there too. Some of the biggest ones."

He gave her a knowing smile. "I'd bet you're another would-be starlet with glamorous, X-rated dreams. Not just a struggling screenwriter." He didn't sound mocking, but he also wasn't trying to be nice. Since handing her the lilies and following her up the stairs, he had withdrawn from her, made her feel like a nettling distraction during his worship session of the great Martedi's brilliant work. It seemed she was jealous of everyone.

Or else in love with them. Probably both. *This* was her natural state. There seemed little chance of overcoming these tendencies without years of intense therapy, which she had always stayed away from, despite her mother's longstanding Tuesday-morning appointments with Dr. Pearse, her roommate's wan little crush on her fifty-six-year-old shrink, her film-school friends' similar dependence on doctors with quiet voices, framed art-exhibition posters, and encouraging, rapacious gazes.

After close to forty minutes of worship, Barrett finally steered her to a cheapish dim sum place on Canal Street where her first embarrassing question was, "Why do you like Lidia so much? How long have you even known her?"

He took a long time to reply. "Your grandfather wasn't faithful to her. Did you know that?"

She hadn't but it wasn't much of a surprise. She doubted that he had been faithful to anyone for more than a few months. How exhausting, she thought. Perhaps this was why she couldn't write a good script. She lacked the necessary libido, the mercenary appetite to consume whatever beautiful things she encountered. Or else be consumed by them. "You didn't answer my question," she said.

"You asked me two questions."

"Yes, if you want to be technical."

"I've known her for a little more than six years. I like her for the same reasons you do. You know what they are."

"Did you ever date her?"

He shook his head and smiled. "I'm too young for her. She likes older men, in case you hadn't noticed."

"She likes men, period."

"Let's not talk about her. She's not here to defend herself," he said, giving her a foxy smile. "You're the most insecure girl I've met in a while who really has no reason to be. You have to stop this, otherwise the next thing you know, you'll wake up and find yourself voting Republican."

"That won't ever happen," she snorted. "No matter how insecure I get."

"You swear?"

"I swear." She looked down at the oil droplets on her plate, wanting to smear them with a fingertip. "I have one more question about Lidia. If you've been friends with her for six years, why weren't you ever in my grandfather's studio before today?"

"You know why."

She shook her head. "He let people visit him there."

"Not many, and I wasn't one of them. I was Lidia's friend, not his. That's definitely how he saw it."

He said this without bitterness. Around age fifteen, she had figured out that her grandfather could have peed on an adoring fan's foot and been excused for his delightful eccentricity. He had known this too but had rarely been mean-spirited. Just self-indulgent, which was his natural state. Along with a maniacal need to be the best and most.

"He gave me three of his sketchbooks just before the accident," she told Barrett a few hours later. She knew it was a stupid thing to do, but at the moment she was overflowing with languid generosity. He had done the same things to her that he had on the night of the bacchanal, the results just as terrific. The torturers of the world had it all wrong, she realized. It was earthshaking sex that would make the enemy confess, not having their toenails ripped off. "There's work in these books that's unlike any of his other stuff."

Barrett said nothing for several seconds. When he finally spoke, he had turned onto his side and was squinting at her as if into a bright light. "I'd really like to see them."

"I'm sure you would. Everyone would. But he was kind of cryptic about what he wanted me to do with them, aside from saying that I should never sell them."

"April," he said quietly. "If you're going to tell me this, I have to think that you want me to see them. Otherwise you're just being cruel."

"I don't mean to be."

"I wouldn't steal his ideas, if that's what you're worried about." He paused, putting a warm hand on her naked belly. "Are they here with you? Or back in California?"

She had brought them with her, afraid of leaving something so valuable with her roommate, even though Monica did not know they existed. "I'm not telling," she whispered, smiling.

"What can I do to get you to show them to me?" he said. "Anything. I'll do anything you want."

This was the most breathtaking thing she had heard in months. His bedroom was dark, but his face glowed, almost radioactive in the charcoal light from one small window above the bed. She could see that he really didn't lie, just as he had boasted on the night they met. "I need to think that over," she finally said.

"Did you love your grandfather?" he asked, exasperated. "You don't always seem to."

"He was a wolf in lion's clothing, like you probably are," she said, suddenly exhausted. "Yes, of course I loved him."

He shook his head. "I'm a mouse in housecat's clothing. If I were like your grandfather, I wouldn't still be living in this shit hole with a growing pile of unsold canvases."

"Great minds seek out greater minds. You're on the right track. Don't feel sorry for yourself."

"Tell me what I can do to get you to show them to me."

"I really don't know if it's a good idea. He didn't want me to show them to anyone."

"Whatever you do, you should give them to a museum. They need to be preserved before they start to deteriorate. Depending on how old they are, they might already be at risk."

"I want you to tell me the real reason why you're bothering with me. That's what I want. Am I here only because you're a huge fan of my grandfather? Tell me the truth."

He looked at her. "No, that's not it at all. You have no reason to doubt me."

"I have no reason to count on you either."

"I suppose that's true," he said slowly. His gray eyes were opaque in his strangely glowing face. "I saw you and I wanted you. That's all there is to it. You're lovely and awkward and unkind to yourself. You have even more to learn than I do. I don't know why you live out in L.A. when most of your friends are here. Hollywood's such a depressing place. The sun only makes it worse. You can't even be in a bad mood without feeling guilty. You need to move back east. We might be rude but at least we're sane. You can write your screenplays here and sell them through an agent." He pulled her to his chest, his dark fur tickling her back. "You must know someone here who can help you out. Your grandfather had to have known a few people who could get things going for you."

"I've never let myself use his name to sell my work. I don't plan on starting either."

"But you should," he said, vehement. "Don't be so proud. There's too much competition not to use whatever connections you've got. Everyone else does. It doesn't mean you're not talented if you ask for help."

This was the same argument her mother had made many times. It was the argument she had with herself whenever she sold nothing and couldn't find anything but menial jobs at the movie studios that made the extravagant garbage consistently befouling the local cineplexes. She was stubborn and vain and could not admit that her lunatic's boat might not get to the top of the mountain, that she might be irrevocably mediocre, despite being the offspring of a genius mother who had sprung from a genius father. Hers seemed on its way to becoming an old dull story, a tale of privilege and not enough early suffering or hungry, single-minded striving or whatever it was that turned a child into a great artist. She persisted in proudly limiting herself, refusing to force her work into production with her grandfather's clout. He had approved of her restraint but had offered to help her anyway. But then had been pleased when she had refused. "No one helped me," he had agreed. "I kept working and working and finally a few people started to notice. If you keep working very hard you'll eventually get what you want and it'll be worth that much more to you." So now, as her mother complained, she was too cowardly to ignore this questionable advice and use his connections. What did it matter if she would only be disappointing a ghost?

She pulled away from Barrett and closed her eyes. The pillowcase smelled stale. She wondered how often he changed the sheets. He was less glamorous than she had expected, and a little nicer; he did not seem at all to be the scoundrel Lidia had warned her he was.

"Show me the notebooks," he whispered. "They're going to change my life. I'm sure of it."

"I don't have them with me."

"Yes, you do. They're at Lidia's. If they weren't, you would have already told me."

She sighed. "Maybe, maybe not."

"All right," he murmured, resigned. "Sleep on it and we'll talk in the morning."

He started softly snoring after a few minutes, but for once she could not sleep. She lay next to him for a long time before creeping slowly from the bed, not wanting to have to explain that she was going back to Lidia's, that she didn't think she should show him the notebooks. He seemed painfully like herself—disappointed in the slow progress of his career, the poverty of his chances as they had so far manifested themselves. But there remained that one significant difference between them—she had the great sheltering bulk of her grandfather's reputation and friendships, if she chose to use them, whereas Barrett did not. Lidia of course had helped him, had gotten him the show in Chelsea where four of his paintings had sold, but so far had been unable to do more for him. As could only happen once, his paintings had arrived on the New York art scene and were now subject to its ruthless whims and upheavals. April also knew that they weren't yet good enough. She suspected he knew this too. He was serious enough about his work to recognize its limitations.

In her grandfather's studio he had said that she seemed surprisingly uninterested in the beauty around her. She had told him that she was not uninterested, only used to it. As far as he was concerned, he said, this was the same thing. She had grown impatient and complained that she was just tired and had been sorting through the studio for days, trying to decide with her mother and Lidia if they would be making a mistake if they released the five remaining portraits from *A Few of the People I've Made Cry* to his gallery. She and Lidia thought it had been Martedi's secret hope, but Beatrice wasn't at all sure. April had said that after she died, no one would have this kind of conversation about her. She had tried to make it into a joke, but the two older women had looked at her and said that at twenty-five she had no reason to indulge in such perverse self-pity.

Barrett might have been having similar thoughts but he at least knew not to voice them. On the way to the restaurant, he told her that according to Lidia, Martedi hadn't made any new work the year before he died. He also hadn't been able to sleep without pills.

No one had told her this. "I knew he had trouble sleeping sometimes," was all she could think to say.

"I assumed that he hit rough patches like every other artist, but apparently this last year was the worst of his life."

"He didn't kill himself, if that's what you're thinking," she blurted. "He would never have considered it."

"I never thought that," said Barrett, taken aback. She felt her face burn with a furious blush and couldn't meet his eyes. "I just think it's very sad that we didn't have one more year of his work before he died," he said quietly.

She was thinking of this exchange, embarrassed by how ignorant and defensive she must have seemed, when she slunk out of his building and walked the block to a vacant taxi stand. The subway was a block farther and she walked toward it, knowing this was a stupid thing to do alone at four in the morning but also knowing that no one would dare attack her in the mood of self-loathing she had plunged into. She was embarrassed by her cowardly flight from his place to Lidia's where she imagined the older woman would answer the bell and look at her with serene disapproval and tell her that she might have been wrong to say that Barrett was unreliable. Or else that she had been wrong about her, the spoiled granddaughter of a great man who at least had not pretended what he did and did not want.

When the subway rumbled into the deserted station, she stepped onto a car where five people were already seated, three of them in maintenance grays, chins tucked against their chests, trying to sleep a little more before starting their unending work. She knew that she would have to show him the notebooks. With little hope, he had been waiting for this.

Twelve

+

Twelve

Someone in the alley three stories below my window was calling out to someone else and what he was saying was not very nice. Maybe he did it because we were all stuck in an ugly, listless March, ice visible everywhere and clinging to our lawns like a dense gray scum. We were exhausted and cynical under cloudy skies, our pants cuffs perpetually caked in grit and mud, our car tires spinning and spinning on snow-choked streets. No one I knew was outside digging up the flower beds, and certainly no one was in the mood to offer spare coins to strangers distractedly ransacking their pockets for change to feed the meters. Instead, people were talking heatedly into mobile phones or looking down at their feet as they trudged, these unloved husbands and crash-dieters and stubborn musicians and disbarred lawyers who all huddled in on themselves because among their other hardships, winter hadn't yet ended and at this near-unendurable point, they just couldn't look each other in the face.

Griggs was in my kitchen on a Saturday morning, sitting right by the window with his coffee and *Tribune,* listening to an outraged someone down in the alley yell insults at a hapless someone else. I was in the other room and didn't hear anything, but when I appeared before him with my newly clean hair and skin, generally pleased with myself, Griggs smiled a little, shook his head and told me what he'd heard. He wouldn't say the obscenities because he was my father's friend and therefore a supposed role model. I looked at him dead-on, repeating what he'd said, adding the missing words. He didn't flinch or give me a disapproving look; he only nodded, as if expecting this. His daughter, born five years after I was, had died a year earlier while living in Spain. Four months after her funeral, he had started calling me because I was a girl, as he said, who had always impressed him with her maturity and self-possession. I was also a nurse, which was something I imagined that he felt he needed. He was divorced, and over the past seven years, had had a series of unsatisfactory girlfriends, some of whom had badmouthed him to his friends, disliked and possibly mistreated his cats (Harriet and Softie), rolled their eyes over his incessant chatter about Shakespeare whose plays and poems he had taught for several years in a night class at a local university, made fun of his old, rusting car and teased him about his hairy, hairy chest.

I had no idea where he had found these women or why he had been attracted to them. I didn't ask too many questions about my predecessors because I felt poorly equipped to handle the answers. At the hospital I had to spend most of the day asking patients questions that they often provided saddening answers for. In my private life, I had gotten into the habit of avoiding similar exchanges. But I knew the answer to one question I wasn't going to ask. The answer was yes. Griggs loved me. I loved him too, but I wasn't saying so to him or anyone else yet. Up until a few months ago, I had only thought of him as my father's friend and then after his daughter's death, my father's stricken friend—a kind, steadily aging presence; a shy joke-teller; a Christmas giver-of-books, usually about or by Shakespeare; a distance runner until his knees gave up; a former husband of the tall and busty LouAnne; a grieving father who would probably always be grieving (I expected nothing else) in some corner of his beaten heart.

He had met my father in college, when he was a sophomore and my father a senior. They had been in the same fraternity and both had almost been recruited for the basketball team. Griggs had turned to running and my father had turned to the commodities market at which he had proven extremely successful—he had retired at forty-two, whereas Griggs had kept doggedly working away at his consulting job until he had amassed enough money and contacts to start his own small consulting firm, which meant that he could manage more and travel less. He was wealthy but was not openly impressed by this fact. His car really was rusting and eleven years old; he lived in a two-bedroom condominium that had no remarkable features; at the time of his divorce, he had given his four-bedroom house with its two-car garage and half-acre lot on the North Shore to LouAnne.

"What do you think inspires people to say such horrible things to each other?" he asked, looking down at the alley which was empty now except for the usual jumble of overturned garbage cans. He was dressed in a white-and-blue-striped button-down and a pair of jeans, his hair damp from the shower he had taken before mine. Weeks ago he had stopped looking as paternal to me as he once had. He was fifty-four and I was thirty. The age difference was not so bad when I thought of it as twelve plus twelve, rather than two dozen or the daunting, flat penalty of twenty-four.

"Habit, maybe?" I said.

He shook his head. "Whatever it is, I wish we could get rid of it."

"Yes, and right after that we'll do in AIDS and cancer."

"I'd like to think that's possible too," he said.

I could have been gentler with him, and for the first couple of months that we had been seeing each other, I had been, exceedingly so. More than once he had awoken in the middle of the night and sat stiffly upright, tears coursing down his face. I would coax him back down and he would lie stiffly next to me, abject and wordless, while I stroked his hair and kissed his face and mouth. *You're recovering from a war,* I had said one night. *You're not yourself and won't be yourself again for a little while longer.* The war was being fought internally, of course, and when I told him something I had started to believe not long before he had arrived in my private life—that people love a good tragedy, provided it doesn't happen to them—he had agreed. It's always easier to manage someone else's pain, he had said.

His daughter Trish, his only child, was living in Seville when she was killed. She had worked for an international organization that sought to reconcile Christians and Muslims. A man, a Spaniard, had died with her, and Griggs had paid the expenses of his funeral too, though the wreck had not been Trish's fault; they had been hit by a drunk driver at two in the morning on their way home from Malaga, where they had been meeting with an imam who was trying to preach religious tolerance in his mosque. Trish had been loved by many in Seville and her friends had held a memorial service for her there. In Chicago, her parents had arranged for another. I had gone to the one in Chicago and had let Griggs hold me for a long time at the door; my father had witnessed this but had said nothing about it until a few weeks later. "I trust you know how upset he was," my father had said. "Still is. He's not functioning the way he normally would. He called here yesterday and asked for your number. You do what you think you should."

That was all he said and it took Griggs three and a half months to dial my number. For weeks we only talked on the phone but then he asked me to dinner and I knew right away what he was up to. It didn't bother me. In fact, I was interested, but at the time, it had all seemed very abstract, as if whatever happened would only be theoretical. I would learn from this and be someone with him I hadn't been with past lovers. My father had some idea what was going on but he didn't ask. My mother knew exactly what was happening but hadn't filled my father in. She said I was old enough to do as I wished, and so was Griggs. But if I wanted to marry and have children, I might want to find someone closer to my age. I had told her that I was in no rush for marriage or for kids, that I liked Griggs quite a lot, and for now, things were fine as they were.

He could not take his eyes off of the alley. The *Tribune* lay unread on his lap. "I've heard people yelling at each other down there before," I said. "It happens pretty often."

"Don't you ever want to call out to them? Tell them to stop?"

"Once in a while, but they're not always swearing at each other."

"I suppose not." He looked at me, opened his mouth then closed it.

"What?"

He shook his head. "Nothing."

"What? You have to tell me now."

He hesitated, his brown eyes not meeting mine. "You could come live with me, if you ever got tired of this."

I was startled but tried not to show it. We had never talked about this. "Thanks, but I'm okay here, sweetie. It's very nice of you to offer though." *Sweetie. Dear. Honey.* These were the words I used with my patients and now with Griggs. I think he liked them too.

He still didn't meet my eyes. ". . . all right, Brynne. I just want you to know that you'd be welcome."

I felt sad for him, but knew that he wouldn't have liked this. For a year now, plenty of people had felt sad for him, and many would never stop. He wanted to forget what had happened. He didn't want to forget Trish, but I think he wanted to forget that he hadn't seen her in almost a year before she died, to forget that he would never see her again. Over the past few months, I might have become the most important person in his life, and it was an oddly humbling thing to know that you mattered, that you were a favorite, possibly irreplaceable. We had been seeing each other for a little less than four months. We now spent three or four nights together each week. I'm not sure why I wasn't more open with my own parents about this.

One of the main reasons, I suppose, was that my father would never have been able to look at either of us the same way again. Maybe he would have started to dislike Griggs. Having lost his own daughter, Griggs was now taking his friend's. I could imagine my father seeing it this way. He was someone who liked ownership, someone who liked knowing exactly where the boundary lines had been drawn; he was not the kind of man other people fooled with either because along with having an incendiary temper, he was physically imposing. Griggs was too, in a way, but he was thinner, less fierce-eyed, and rarely did he seem to overwhelm whatever room he walked into. It wasn't like he and my father would have gotten into a fistfight, but I knew that Griggs worried about my father's reaction. Yet, inviting me to live with him indicated a new willingness to make our affair much more public.

"I'd better get going," he said, setting the newspaper on the table next to his coffee cup. "I'm supposed to have lunch with LouAnne today."

This didn't bother me; they were friends and after twenty years of marriage, it seemed a sensible thing to be. What bothered me was that it was only ten a.m. "You could stay a little longer," I said. "I'm not due at the hospital until two."

"No, I'd better go. I have to do some grocery shopping that I've been putting off all week."

"I'll see you tomorrow night?"

He nodded. "I'll be home around seven if that's still good."

"I could come to you. Your cats wouldn't have to be alone again."

of our relationship. He would surely die before me, possibly long before. Or he assumed I would leave him when he started to look like an old man. And not yet having told him I loved him, maybe he didn't think I did. As the one supposedly with more options and less vulnerability, he might have thought that I should be the one to take the risk and say it first.

Fuck you, asshole! These incredible words, arriving in my head unbidden, made me laugh out loud—how horrible, how absurd, ever to say them to him!

I had trouble falling asleep, and in the morning, the phone woke me unceremoniously at eight o'clock. My first witless thought—Griggs was calling to apologize for last night, and I answered without checking the caller ID. It wasn't him. Instead, a woman, and at first I couldn't place her voice, but then I realized with a guilty jolt that the voice belonged to LouAnne. She said good morning very cheerfully, not acknowledging the sleep in my froggy hello, asked about my parents, and then in one almost indecipherably fast sentence said she wanted to know if I would like some of Trish's things. She had slowly been cleaning out her room over the past few months, and Griggs had already taken what he wanted. She thought that I might like some of Trish's books and some of her sweaters and blouses too because we were about the same size. "Unless you've shrunk or grown lately?" she said with a laugh. Parceling out her daughter's things to friends seemed to her a much better idea than giving everything to the Goodwill. "I'd like the people who knew Trish to keep her more tangibly in their lives," she said. "I hope you don't think that's too morbid."

"No, not at all. It's very kind of you to offer." I had no idea what else to say. She had to have known that Trish and I hadn't been very close; surely her daughter had had other friends who would have wanted her things. But it seemed very unkind to turn LouAnne down because how to decline a grieving mother's offer without seeming rude and insensitive?

Yet I knew that more had to be going on here. I knew that she had some idea of how long Griggs and I had been seeing each other. At yesterday's lunch, in a snit over the move-in offer I had turned down, maybe Griggs had said more about me to her than he had needed to. Was she jealous? Seven years post-divorce?

It wasn't unlikely. In her view, I supposed, I was much too young for him and still capable of entrapping men in their twenties and thirties, so

"They're fine. They have each other." He paused, looking a little anxious. "Every other night isn't too hard on them, is it?"

"I'm not sure, but I really wouldn't mind staying at your place more. You don't have an alley either." I smiled, standing on my toes to kiss him goodbye. He put his arms around me and hugged me hard. He hadn't shaved, and his whiskers pricked my forehead.

"I'll miss you tonight," he murmured.

"I'll miss you too."

When he left, I felt a disorienting mix of loneliness and relief. We were a funny pair, I knew, people often eyeballing us when we went out. *What's going on there?* I could almost hear them whispering. *Is she a gold digger or what?* His daughter and I had liked each other but had only been acquaintances. I had already graduated from college before she started her freshman year. As kids, we had lived several towns apart and had only seen each other on rare occasions. Even so, as an adult, I had been interested in keeping up with her; her politics had impressed me, as had her fluency in Spanish, and her willingness to live in a foreign country where she helped to keep dangerous strangers from murdering each other. My closest girlfriend, a nurse too, thought it was creepy that Griggs and I were lovers—"Don't you think it's all a little incestuous?" she had asked early on. "Don't you think he's a little weird? Why did he start calling you? What's he trying to do? Pretend that you're her when you're together?"

I didn't think any of this, at least not anymore. He was genuinely curious about my life, my opinions, my desires; we rarely talked about Trish and he had once said that he had started thinking about me a few years before her death, inappropriate as I probably found this to be. Still, I understood my friend's concerns. At first I had wondered the same things about him. I had worried that he would try to get me to dye my hair to match Trish's or learn more Spanish or that he would accidentally call me by her name. But nothing like that had happened. He and I were adults, as my mother had said. We were a couple, one whose future together was as unpredictable as most couples'.

That afternoon, I went to work and no one I had been taking care of the day before in the ICU had died or else been upgraded to non-critical care. I had two elderly male stroke victims and a young woman who had fallen down some stairs and badly injured her spine. There was also a new admit, a teenage boy who had been in a car accident, his jaw now wired shut, both eyes so swollen with contusions that he couldn't see. His mother was with him and planned to stay for as much time as she was allowed. His father was in California, on business, and wasn't able to get back until tomorrow. The boy's mother told me this with obvious bitterness, while her son, body and jaw immobilized, could do nothing but groggily listen. I touched her hand and said it was a shame. I touched his hand gently too, checking his IVs; we had him on glucose and morphine drips. I also had to make sure his catheter was still in place; this was delicate work, especially with a fuming, stricken mother waiting on the other side of the door. Few mothers wanted to think about a youngish nurse poking around their sons' precious genitals, but the good news was this boy's semi-conscious state. His parents could not yet understand their luck, such as it was. Many patients weren't far from a coma when first admitted to my unit, and the only exit for some was through the back door, which once shut could not be opened again.

The name on the boy's chart was Mark McGinnis, his DOB showing him to be only a few weeks away from seventeen, both eyes bloodied plums, his mouth and cheeks bruised and lacerated too. He had spanked the windshield hard with his face and suffered a concussion. Seven of his ribs had been cracked against the steering wheel. He had crushed a knee-cap and broken a femur, both wrists and his collarbone too. He had not been wearing his seat belt in an old car, one without an airbag. But he had not died. It wouldn't have been good bedside manner, but I wanted to say this to his mother who right then was more interested in hating his father. Mark was going to survive all of his injuries and perhaps be a humbler person, a better driver, a nicer guy. He would not forget this, any of it, not for a very long time.

I had seen hundreds of car crash victims. Like diabetics, cancer sufferers, and pregnant women, they kept hospitals in gurneys and syringes. Despite all of the crash patients, I hadn't really thought about the particulars of Trish's wreck until Griggs and I started seeing each other. What he didn't know was that I could picture her; whether I wanted to or not, I could see the paramedics, the ambulance, her bloody, ruined body as they rushed her to the hospital. I had heard from my father that her neck had been snapped on impact, her chest crushed, her vital organs arrested under terrible pressure. That Griggs did not have the ability to see her as I could was clearly a blessing, and perhaps this was why I had first wanted

to be near him. I could imagine something he shouldn't ever be allowed to imagine, and I wanted to protect him from it.

At eleven p.m. when my shift ended, Mark was in the care of the night nurses, and his mother went home for a few hours. I returned to my pet-less, chilly apartment and missed my boyfriend, which seemed a ridiculous word to use for a man in his fifties. His *Tribune* still sat on the table next to his half-full coffee mug. By now, he was probably sleeping; Sunday night was hardly the most animated time of the week, except sometime for the ER staff with their end-of-weekend crop of desperate cases.

I ate a bowl of cereal and took a shower, my second of the day which I knew wasn't a good idea because it dried out the skin and brought o wrinkles faster, but I could smell the hospital in my hair, and tonight didn't want to carry it into my sleep. Afterward, in bare feet and a war robe, I went into the kitchen and was pouring myself a glass of wat when through the old windows overlooking the alley I heard two peop shouting.

Fuck you, asshole!

Fuck you too, you asshole's asshole!

I peered down at them, keeping the lights off. Two men, one ol possibly a father and son. The older one was gesticulating aggressiv lunging forward and giving the other guy the bird with both middle gers. The younger guy waved him off and disappeared around the cor For some reason, the older guy didn't go after him. He dropped his ha turned slowly on his heel and walked the other way. I called Griggs, v him up and told him what I had seen. "Do you need me to come over" asked sleepily.

"No, no. I just thought you'd get a kick out of it."

"You could have saved it until tomorrow. I would have gotten a kic of it then too."

"I might have forgotten to tell you."

"I doubt that." He yawned.

I told him that I was sorry to have woken him. He said not to about it. Hanging up, I felt irritated. Disappointed too. I had wante to insist on coming over. Not long ago, I knew he would have.

Perhaps I had begun the process of losing him. Maybe by not I would live with him or even consider it, I had made him thin harder than any time before now, about the impracticalities, the b

what the hell was I doing with a man in her age group? Let alone the father of her only, now-lost child?

But to offer me Trish's things seemed an odd way for her to remind me of my place in the dating hierarchy.

"If you have a little time this week, why don't you come over and take a look at what's here?" she said.

I wanted to put her off indefinitely but didn't know how. "If it's all right with you," I said, "next weekend would probably be better for me."

"How about Saturday morning if you're not working?"

We settled on Saturday. She didn't say a word about Griggs and me, but the two of us must have been in her head, making some kind of trouble. Maybe I was a self-absorbed fool to think that she spent much time worrying about Griggs and disliking me, but I felt sure that next Saturday would not be a blue-sky-white-puffy-cloud kind of day. I could already feel something combative and defiant rearing up in me.

I had the day off, having worked until 11 the previous night, and I spent the morning cleaning and then trying to read a library book. At one o'clock when Griggs usually took his lunch break, I called and told him about LouAnne's offer. Of the two of us, I was the only one surprised.

"She asked me what I thought at lunch yesterday," he said. "I told her that she should do as she saw fit."

"You don't think it's a little strange?"

He hesitated. "Well, yes, maybe a little. Do you even want any of Trish's things?"

"I don't know. Maybe if I weren't dating her father. It seems like LouAnne is trying to remind us that you could be my father too."

For a few long seconds, he didn't reply. "We can't all be as closely matched as Romeo and Juliet."

"That's a good thing, considering how they ended up."

"*Desire my pilot is, beauty my prize.* That's from *Lucrece.*"

"Never heard of it."

"Not many have. It's one of Shakespeare's first poems."

"I don't want to go over there on Saturday."

"Then don't. Tell her you've had second thoughts. She'll understand."

"I bet she'll be offended. Wouldn't you be?"

"No, I don't think so, but I probably wouldn't have asked you either.

Sorry about this, Brynne." He exhaled audibly. "I can talk to her if you'd like."

It seemed risky to let him, but better than confronting her myself. "If you wouldn't mind," I said. Whatever was going on here was between them anyway, but I hadn't realized this until now.

We said nothing more about it that night when he came over, nor on Wednesday, the next night we stayed together, me at his place this time where I insisted his cats sleep with us, poor Softie and Harriet purring half the night, unable to believe their good luck at having two warm human bodies to huddle close to. On Friday I finally asked him if he had talked to LouAnne and he said that he had. "She understood. I knew she would. It would have been an awkward thing for you, obviously. She did understand this."

"I sometimes wonder why you two got divorced."

He gave me a wry smile. "I've told you why. We were like an adolescent brother and sister. Lots of arguments and certainly no sex."

"Someday that could happen to us."

He shook his head. "I won't live that long."

"Please don't say that," I said, my eyes closing involuntarily. "I don't like to think of either of us dying."

"Neither do I, but I do it anyway. What happened to that boy you've been taking care of? The one with all those broken bones?"

I hadn't kept Mark McGinnis and his car wreck from Griggs because he asked about my patients all the time, wanting to know their circumstances, what I had to do for them, who visited and brought along magazines and stuffed bears. I couldn't lie about any of this. He seemed to know that Trish's death, the way it had arrived, was unremarkable—except in its impact on those who had loved her. This seemed true of most deaths, as the hospital and its beggar's trade made clear to me every day. But I loved the place anyway. I loved knowing that many people, if not everyone, recovered. Some were better, more alive and hopeful, when they left than they had been at any other time in their lives.

"They moved him out of ICU a few days ago," I said. "His orthopede said he's healing well. He's very young so he'll heal fast. They'll probably let him go home in another week, but he's in for months of physical therapy. He'll have to use a cane for a while after he starts walking again but eventually he won't need it."

"That's very good news."

"He'll be fine, I think. I've heard his friends are coming to see him now that we've got him in a regular bed. That always helps."

"His whole life," he murmured, "is wide open and waiting for him."

I looked at him, at his kind, serious face. We were sitting across from each other at the kitchen table and I reached over to touch his hand. "Well, yes, it is," I said.

He smiled. "You're very good at what you do."

I wasn't sure what he meant. "Thank you, I try."

"You're succeeding."

When we were in bed later, in the sleepy, expansive time that followed sex, I lifted my head from his shoulder and told him I loved him, not wanting to keep it from him any longer. He looked at me and smiled as if wonderfully sad, saying he loved me too. "Very much, Brynne," he said. "I'm so glad you feel that way about me. I didn't want to assume."

"You could have," I said, running my fingers through the lavish dark hair that covered his chest.

"I'm not much of a gambler anymore. Maybe that's not such a good thing in this case." He paused. "I'm sorry about the whole thing with LouAnne. You must have wanted to clobber me."

"It was strange, but it wasn't your fault."

"I didn't know what to say when she asked me."

"No would probably have been best," I teased. "But really, it's okay."

The next day, Saturday, Griggs went into the office to work on his quarterly budget before we met up again for the night. I was baking a chocolate cake after craving one all week when the front-door buzzer barged into my apartment. On the intercom was the same female voice that had woken me at eight the previous Monday morning. "It's me, LouAnne Griggs," she cried. After a dry-mouthed, sucked-in second of panic, I buzzed her up, too dimwitted to think of a way to fend her off.

She had a plastic bag in her hand, a lump-filled bag that contained some things I did not want to see, let alone keep. I couldn't really believe this bad news, as if someone had just handed me a thousand-dollar fine for stealing a pistachio from the bulk foods bin.

Nonetheless, I think she felt as nervous as I did, her face flushed, her eyes darting around the living room where I led her to an armchair and offered her something to drink. Either Griggs hadn't talked to her or she had been intent all along on seeing me. The latter seemed most likely; Griggs didn't lie, as far as I could tell. "You have a nice little place," she said. "How long have you lived here?"

"About a year."

"You own it?"

I nodded.

"A good starter home."

"Yes, I suppose so."

She nodded, pretending interest in the black-and-white photos hanging on the walls—enlarged prints from a trip I had taken to Australia several years earlier.

"Paul is very taken with you," she eventually said, her voice uncharacteristically quiet.

"I guess I feel the same about him."

"I thought you might. He's an extremely nice man." She pulled a furry blue cardigan from the bag and held it up. "Our daughter never wore this," she said. "I gave it to her for Christmas a few years ago. I'd keep it if it fit me."

"It's pretty," I said, not really meaning it.

"I think you should have it."

My stomach lurched. I could have cried out in frustration but instead sat docilely, guts churning. "I don't know if Paul told you, but I don't think I can accept any of Trish's things."

"She liked you, Brynne. I used to think you two should get together more, but I know the age difference made it a little difficult."

"Yes, I suppose it did." I tried to smile. "You're very kind to offer me her things, but I really don't think I can take them."

"Because of you and Paul," she said flatly.

"That's part of it, yes."

"I need to say something to you, sweetie."

I looked at her, waiting, not trusting the endearment. The whine of a motor started up outside. A leaf blower, I thought, not a lawnmower, not yet.

"If he asks you to marry him, don't say yes unless you plan to stay with him. If he marries you and you divorce him a year or two later, I don't think he'll survive it."

I stared at her. "We've never discussed marriage. We've only been together for a few months."

"Doesn't matter," she said, shaking her head. "I can see it coming." She reached into the bag again, pulling out a fistful of sweaters. "I want you to take one of Trish's tops. Just one. You can pick it out. I brought eight or nine."

Out of shock more than guilt, I finally agreed. I worried that she would have sat in my living room all day waiting for me to change my mind. She nodded with stern approval when I chose a lavender pullover, cable-knit, very pretty, but I doubted I would ever wear it. Trish probably hadn't worn it either; I had never seen her in pastels, nor in lipstick or eyeshadow. Of the two of us, I had always worn the make-up and the Easter egg colors.

LouAnne left a few minutes later, apologizing for arriving unannounced. "Paul won't like that I did this," she said at the door. "I imagine you'll tell him. I suppose I would too, but please don't be mad at me."

"I'm not mad," I said.

"Maybe not now, but later you will be." She hugged me stiffly, with one arm, and then she was gone. I stood behind the closed door and let out my breath, my chest and stomach finally relaxing. I had been sweating too, my underarms nearly dripping with it.

I jumped when the oven timer went off, at first thinking it was the door buzzer again. After I pulled out the cake, I sat at the kitchen table and stared out the window, smelling the chocolate but hardly registering it. Cars drove in and out of the alley every few minutes, garage doors creaking open and closed, but there were very few voices, only a crying child, then his harried mother demanding that he hurry up and get into the van. I thought about calling Griggs to tell him about LouAnne, but didn't. I didn't know when I would tell him. I wasn't mad at her. I was surprised and a little chastened, but also a little pleased. It was as if she had called my bluff, one I hadn't known about until now.

After dinner that night and a piece of cake with too much frosting, Griggs said, "I'd like to see Mark McGinnis."

I looked at him for a long time, wondering if this might be a very unwise thing for him to do. I really had no idea, not even a theory. "I suppose I could take you," I finally said. "But I'll have to check to see if it's okay with him."

Griggs considered this in silence.

"I think he'll say yes," I said. "When I tell him about you, he'll probably say yes."

"No, no. Don't tell him about me. Just go by his room tomorrow and I'll follow you and you can go in and say hello. I'll poke my head in and pretend that I'm looking for you. That's all I want. Just to see him."

I had started crying but his eyes were dry. He looked purposeful, not desperate or bereft. "Are you sure you really want to do that?" I asked, my voice breaking.

"Oh Brynne, don't— Please don't cry. I'm fine. I just want to see him. Nothing else. I won't try to befriend him or anything. I promise it'll be okay. I just want to see him for myself."

He kept looking at me calmly, and eventually I heard myself say yes. "I suppose you could come by tomorrow afternoon."

"That'll work," he said. "I won't do anything but say hello. Then I'll leave."

"If you're sure you really want to do this?"

"Yes, I'm sure."

We planned for him to meet me during my lunch hour. I agreed to walk down the hall on the third floor in the east wing with him several steps behind me, watching silently as I turned into Mark's room. With heart pounding, I would do it. I would do this for him and afterward, I knew that I would hold onto him in the hallway, not caring if other nurses or doctors were questioning the propriety of such a display. One or both of us would start crying and eventually we would have to stop. Not long after, he would leave and I would go back to work and we would both be different. We would see each other differently from then on, as if we had been in a speeding car heading toward another speeding, unsteady car, but somehow it hadn't swerved from its lane and hit us. Somehow we had been allowed to drive on without incident, down the rest of the highway, right to our street and into the garage. We had locked the car and walked into the house, and everything was there, the hall light burning, the curtains closed—everything was just as we had left it.

You're

So

Different

Over the past two hours, she has heard a number of very personal complaints from people she knew twenty years ago, most of whom she hasn't spoken with since they were in high school together. The hall the party planners have rented is poorly maintained and stinks of rotting wood and damp plaster, the water-stained ceiling flaking in the corners. Tickets, inexplicably, were eighty dollars, but she kept her word, bought her plane ticket as promised, and reserved a hotel room. Three of the organizers had called her office in far away San Jose and begged her to come. For the past nine years, she has been someone to know, her name familiar to people who care about movies. Some of her former classmates have sent letters in the past few years, saying how proud they are of her, offering ideas for future films, scenes from their lives she would never write about without adding something to corrupt the event, to turn it strange and absurd, or else tragic; she knows the changes would offend the letter-writers if she were ever to use their stories—the truth always curiously flat to her before its reworking, no matter how bizarre or scandalous.

She blames her last film for the unsolicited confessions and grievances: the protagonist is an inexperienced psychologist whose patients talk of nothing but their love lives, ones defined by experimentation and cartoonish cruelty.

And now several of Margaret's classmates have offered unwanted confidences, a few of the boldest asking that she go with them to a table where no one else sits, to a quiet corner by the bar, where they ask what she thinks they should say to their wives or husbands who no longer seem to want to touch them or talk to them, who are more interested in their cars or tai chi instructors or the night class where they spend hours looking at naked strangers and badly drawing them. And their children—only fifteen years old and already asking to go on the pill! Why this ferocious desire for the unseemly at such an early age?

She must keep herself from sighing with irritation as she listens, or from laughing, scornful of how inadequate her classmates' memories are—as if they were never curious about sex, of whatever was forbidden, luridly sexy, sold expensively in a nearby city's red light district where few dared to go without a sturdy group of five or six, with their fake, felonious driver's licenses. They look at her with such respect, with such curiosity and hunger, wanting to know all that she knows, to be friends with the actors who have portrayed her characters, to live a life that so many people hope for. She has rarely been the focus of so much breathless attention; in California, she learned early on that for the most part, screenwriters are regarded as little more than grasping know-it-alls. When she mentions this to a woman she remembers faintly from an English class, the woman shakes her head in disbelief. "Without you, how could there be a movie?"

"It's almost always the director's movie, or the producer's," says Margaret.

"How ridiculous," cries the woman. "They don't write the dialogue, do they? The story wasn't theirs to begin with, was it?"

"By the time we're done filming, the script sometimes isn't mine either."

"That's ridiculous," the woman says again. "How can you stand it? I'd go crazy."

Margaret has come alone, her boyfriend, a film historian named Oliver, having refused to travel to Richfield with her because he said, fairly enough, that he would know no one and would be forced to hang uselessly about her for the entire evening. She wishes he had come anyway; she feels exposed, as if she is a freakish sideshow, which is more or less her role for the evening. Oliver would intimidate her classmates with his habit of locking gazes during even the most trivial conversations, and his unfamiliar, handsome face would undoubtedly have deterred the advances of the temporary confessionalists, their eager, inquisitive looks the only discomfort she would have to endure.

It is midway through the evening when the most extravagant embarrassment occurs, one that she knows is expected to please her, though it seems only the most desperate flattery. The reunion organizers, three women named Patty, Susan and Birdy, the first of whom is vastly pregnant and tipsy, unveil the night's surprise tribute—a series of clips excerpted from Margaret's five films and arranged to a melodramatic effect so excessive that she sneaks out of the hall just before the screening ends but then is intercepted in the parking lot by a man whom she recognizes as someone she once admired for his trombone playing and long, muscular legs.

"It's not a fun party, is it." He smiles, apologetic. "I couldn't believe that you bothered with it. With us."

She crosses her arms over her chest, the air chilly for early August. "I didn't make it to the one ten years ago."

"I did. I promised myself afterwards that I wouldn't go to any of the other ones."

"Then how did this happen?"

"I'm married to Birdy."

Margaret looks at him, trying to hide her surprise. "Cornell, right?" He is not wearing a nametag, the clip-on one everyone was given at check-in with senior year pictures pasted to the left of each name.

"Yes, Maggie Rieger. Do you remember my last name too?"

She hesitates. "It starts with an H, doesn't it?"

"It starts with an S-C-H. Schweitzer."

He follows her deeper into the parking lot, watching as she takes the keys to her rental car out of her handbag and tugs on the shoulder strap of her dress, feeling awkward beneath his interested gaze. "Birdy and I got married two years ago," he continues. "I was married once before. So was she. But not to each other." He laughs. "I suppose that's obvious."

"Not necessarily."

"Oh, that's right. In California they must do it all the time."

She does not like this sort of generalization and often reprimands the people who make them, but Cornell is ill at ease, as is she, though she suspects that she has whatever advantage is to be had. He is handsome, tall and lean, one long-fingered hand reaching out to touch her forearm. "Maggie," he says quietly. "Birdy and I wanted to invite you to dinner at our place tomorrow night. I know we haven't kept in touch, but we thought it would be nice. We both love your movies. Though I probably love them a little more than she does."

She grips her keys, feeling them bite into her palm. "I'd like to have dinner with you," she lies, "but my flight leaves at four o'clock tomorrow afternoon."

His face falls but he quickly recovers himself. "How about lunch then? I'm sure Birdy and I could manage that."

She wants to say no, that she has urgent work to do, a deadline in a week or a treatment to write for Monday morning, but she can't lie to him. He is someone she has rarely thought about in twenty years, though at one time, she had liked and admired him, thinking him funny and sharp and possibly destined for greatness because his talent for music had been an established fact—he could claim a certain distinction in a class of 198, only half of the graduates having gone on to any kind of college in the autumn after graduation.

"I could probably drop by for a little while," she says, startled when he grasps both of her forearms, squeezing them almost too hard.

"That's wonderful, Maggie. I promise it'll be much less hectic for you than tonight was." He reaches into a pocket inside his gray suit jacket, pulling out an eelskin billfold. He hands her a pale blue card. "Here's our address. Twelve o'clock tomorrow? Is that all right?"

"Yes, that should be fine."

"If you need directions, give us a call." He pauses. "Do you like sea-food?"

She nods. "Should I bring something?"

"No. You're our guest. We'll take care of everything."

He shakes her hand, bowing his head slightly before returning to the hall that a few couples are now exiting, their laughter jarring against the quiet night. Cornell glances over his shoulder once to find that she is still standing by her car door, staring absently after him. He waves a little and she hurries to unlock the car, embarrassed by her momentary disorientation.

Her parents have long since sold their house and moved south to escape the harsh Midwestern winters. Having lost touch with anyone else in Richfield, she is staying in a mid-grade hotel, the only one that Richfield offers. She learned at the reunion that a second, nicer hotel had closed down two years earlier after it became known that the chef in the hotel restaurant was renting a room off of the kitchen, by the hour, to three prostitutes, one of whom died of a heroin overdose while on the job. The carpet of Margaret's room feels soggy to her bare feet, the air humid from leaky windows. She puts on a T-shirt, brushes her teeth and calls Oliver in San Jose, hoping he is alone for a change; he is often working on a project with one or two research assistants he hires almost without exception from Ivy League schools, all of them male and obsequious at first but eventually so lackadaisical and self-assured that Oliver finds he can no longer work with them.

"What the hell will you talk about with those people?" Oliver says when she tells him of her lunch date with the Schweitzers.

"We'll think of something. It's only for an hour or so."

"If you're lucky."

"What do I say to Birdy if she asks me what I thought about the tribute?"

"Tell her you loved it. Tell her it blew your mind to smithereens. Tell her you found it reductive and demeaning."

"Sure. I'll tell her that."

"You knew you were going to be a show pony tonight. I don't know why you went in the first place."

"I felt like I had to. They kept calling me."

"Did you also feel like you had to have lunch with those people?"

"I sort of knew Cornell in high school. We had a few classes together."

"Cornell?"

"Birdy's husband."

"Birdy and Cornell. There's a pair for you," he says unkindly, taking a drink from what sounds like a beer bottle, though usually he drinks red wine.

"I really don't miss you very much when you say things like that."

"You don't have to miss me. I know you're very busy out there in the heartland."

"You say that like it's a disgrace. If I remember correctly, you grew up in Iowa."

"Yes, but I never go back there. It's all a blur now."

"Don't be mad about the lunch tomorrow."

"I'm not. I'm jealous. I didn't know you in high school like they did."

"You didn't miss anything."

"Women always say that, Margaret. It's false modesty. In truth, you know we've missed a lot." He pauses. "My sons are coming on Thursday. You didn't forget, I hope."

"No, I remember."

"I'd like you to go out to dinner with us after they get here."

"Are you sure they'll want my company?"

"I want your company."

"You should ask them first."

"I'm sure they'll want you to come."

"Please ask them."

He sighs. "All right, I will."

Before they hang up, she tells him she loves him, as she often does, but he pauses so long she thinks she's upset him. Finally, he says, "I'm sorry I didn't go with you. I suppose I should have been more generous. I love you too. Very much, Margaret." Then he hangs up, his goodbyes always abrupt, leaving a hollow in her chest, as if she is seeing someone beloved for the last time from the window of a moving car.

Unable to sleep past six-thirty, she wakes up with a headache and spends most of the morning working on a script she has been hired to write for a wealthy producer, a difficult adaptation of a novel told mainly in convoluted flashbacks, a book she is surprised anyone wants to transform into a movie because its characters are uniformly masochistic and contrary, most of them dying violently before the story's end. In a way, it shames her—her growing penchant for happy endings corrupting her long-standing respect for austerity and her belief that much of life is tragedy tempered by occasional felicitous events, sadness ultimately outweighing joy, the ponderous weight of unhappiness always, by nature, greater than its opposite.

She had thought she might want to spend part of the day driving around town, visiting a park where she used to walk her chubby cocker spaniel Mae in the evening and pass by the house of a Spanish teacher on her way home, a youngish man on whom she had once had an incendiary crush, which he was kind enough to ignore. But now in Richfield, after the awkwardness of the reunion, she feels uninterested in nostalgia and misses her life in San Jose more than she does any person or era from the past when her idea of herself and her talents was still inchoate, the supposed blank slate that turns out already to be half-filled, scribbled across by heredity and the fears of early childhood.

By eleven-thirty she is packed and ready to check out of her room, too soon to drive to Birdy and Cornell's house which is five minutes away. She stops at a grocery store, buying a bouquet of daisies from the floral stand and a large box of chocolate caramels that she hopes Birdy will open before she has to leave for the airport. In California she almost never buys candy; it is a childish indulgence her life as a supposed Hollywood luminary is not meant to allow room for. Her body, like her mind, is expected to be muscular and dazzling, and at best, heartbreaking.

It is still a few minutes before twelve when she arrives at the Schweitzers' house on Mayfair Street, a pretty brick Colonial with a big front yard, tall spruce and maple trees growing close to the edge of their property, lilac bushes lining the driveway. She wonders if they have children, probably from their first marriages, though Birdy is not yet past child-bearing age, and her reunion co-chair Patty's pregnancy was much celebrated the previous night. Margaret has no children and hasn't yet regretted this, her work and her lovers requiring all of her time and energy, as it has been by her design.

She parks her car in front of the house but stays inside until the clock radio reads 12:00, wondering if someone is peering out of the front windows, anxious that she will stand them up, which is a thought that seriously tempted her upon waking—what could they possibly do; what would it matter after a week or two had passed, her feelings of wrongdoing diluted? Her former classmates hold no sway over her life or career, over anything that matters to her, though she has made a point of not becoming a person who lies with such ease that truth and deceit have begun to blend like hot and cold water poured into the same glass, the end result something tepid but bearable.

At the front door, Birdy hugs Margaret tightly, exclaiming over the flowers and the boxed chocolates, Cornell standing behind his wife, his face bearing a strained smile, and when he shakes her hand, his palm is damp, wet enough that she furtively wipes her hand on her skirt as they lead her farther into the house, the air smelling of something sweet baking in the oven. Margaret feels a flash of anxiety, of near-panic, not knowing what they expect from her, why they wanted to invite her to lunch after not knowing her for twenty years.

Birdy's face, however—olive-skinned, as smooth as a woman's in her twenties—is without guile, her dark eyes gazing raptly at Margaret as she and Cornell squire Margaret from room to room on the first floor, waiting for her to praise their lace curtains and polished hardwood floors, the antique rolltop desk and black walnut coffee table, the framed photos of handsome family members on top of bookshelves and the two television sets. In school she didn't know Birdy well; they only had gym classes together, Birdy aggressive in every sport, particularly good at tennis and scornful of those who were less coordinated, but now she is heavier, her body padded at each curve, her earlier aggression having given way to an ambiguous fatigue or disenchantment, possibly at having spent so many years trying to please her parents and then a husband, trying to be exceptional at things that turned out not to matter so much.

"It's so nice that you made time for us today," says Birdy, finally showing Margaret to a table laden with expensive, flower-trimmed dishes and gleaming silverware, a large crystal salad bowl in the middle, filled with tiny shrimp and Boston lettuce. "I know we're not nearly as exciting as Hollywood must be."

Margaret smiles, sitting down on a walnut chair, its seat cushion covered with needlepoint cabbage roses. "What you see in the movie theaters is as exciting as it gets. Most of the parties I'm invited to are embarrassingly stage-managed. It's about the caterers, the music, the wine, the decor, though no one is supposed to say so. I only go to the parties my agent insists that I can't miss."

"Your agent," exclaims Birdy. "I don't know anyone with an agent."

Margaret glances at Cornell, embarrassed to have behaved so predictably, tossing around the casual details of her supposedly glamorous lifestyle. "It's more like she's my business partner."

Birdy passes Margaret a plate filled with shrimp salad, suddenly giving her a stricken look. "Is this all right?" she asks. "Cornell said you like seafood."

"It looks beautiful. I like most things, shrimp included." She takes the plate, setting it down, waiting for Birdy to serve Cornell and herself. After filling the plates, Birdy pours water into three goblets, and iced tea into a second set, passing one of each to Margaret.

They eat in heavy silence for a few moments, Cornell finally looking up and asking, "Did you always want to write screenplays? Why not novels?"

"I didn't think I was good enough to be a novelist," she says slowly. "I still don't know if I'm good enough to be a screenwriter."

"You might never know," says Cornell. "Though you seem to be doing all right so far."

She nods but doesn't reply, her mouth full of salad.

Birdy looks up from her plate. "Have you ever dated an actor?" she asks shyly.

Margaret smiles, a little sheepish. "No one famous. The actor I dated the longest has done a few guest spots on different TV shows, but you probably wouldn't know him if you saw him."

Birdy gazes at her. "I wonder how you ended up somewhere so different from where we are. Your life must be a lot more interesting than ours."

Margaret feels a stab of unease. "I wouldn't say that. My work is different from what most people do, but many other things are the same."

Birdy laughs. "I don't believe you."

Cornell looks from his wife to Margaret but doesn't speak. He takes a long drink of iced tea, setting down his glass with exaggerated care.

"I don't know if I'm any happier now than I was in high school or college," says Margaret.

"But would you trade places with Birdy and me?" asks Cornell. "Don't lie."

His gaze is sharper than she expects. "I suppose it would depend on what you do for a living. If you're still a musician, then I might consider it."

He shakes his head. "That didn't work out. I didn't have enough confidence or passion, I suppose. I went to law school instead. I have my own small practice. Birdy's a registered nurse."

"Cornell," says Birdy, irritated. "You know she wouldn't trade places. I wouldn't."

"You have kids, don't you? I noticed some pictures in the living room," Margaret says, hoping they won't argue in front of her. She realizes with a jolt that they really are strangers, almost as unknown to her as someone off the street.

Birdy nods. "Yes, a boy and a girl from my first marriage. They're with their father in Delavan this weekend. Cornell doesn't have any."

"Do you have kids?" says Cornell.

Margaret shakes her head.

"What about my other question?" he says.

She hesitates, glancing at Birdy who is trying to spear a shrimp with her oversized fork. "I don't think I'd want to trade places with anyone. It's hard to imagine living a life other than the one you have."

He shakes his head. "No, I think it's very easy to imagine what you might have had instead."

"But you still don't know if in the end it will make you happier."

He gives her a look of almost angry challenge. "You could write a screenplay about this and figure it out that way. Dickens seemed to think that Scrooge would have been happier."

She does not know where it has come from, Cornell's sudden pique, his desire to expose and belittle her. Her own family does it often enough, but she understands it in them, their disbelief that she has achieved something meaningful that they haven't directly engineered. That she doesn't need as much from them as she once did.

"I suppose most of my scripts are about possibility. How far your life will take you."

"And they're about sex," murmurs Cornell.

Birdy makes a funny sound and clinks her water glass heavily against her plate.

He looks at his wife. "What? It's true. They are about sex. You've said so yourself more than once."

"Yes, but you make it sound so terrible." She gives Margaret an apologetic look. "We own copies of all of your movies."

"I didn't say that I didn't like them." He chews a bite of salad, his jaw working energetically. He looks at Margaret. "They're excellent movies.

I'm envious. You're ensured a bit of immortality, I imagine. Whatever that's worth."

"They're not only about sex."

"I know. They're also about disappointment and fear of death. And outsmarting your enemies and how money is terribly dirty," says Cornell. "I've learned a lot from them."

She hears what she knows is sarcasm but doesn't know how to respond. She does not throw tantrums—this is the one thing she has refused to do, as an adult, as a woman in the film industry who, against the odds, has become a modest success. "I've always hoped that they were useful for something other than avoiding real life for a couple of hours."

"Never fear," he says. "As long as you're doing your thing, we're safe from complete despair."

"Cornell. Jesus Christ," says Birdy, glaring at him with what looks like real outrage. "What's the matter with you?" To Margaret, she says, "I'm sorry you've had to put up with this. I have no idea what's wrong with him."

He glares at his wife. "You make me sound like a crackpot. I'm only speaking my mind. Margaret can handle it. She must have a leather hide by now, all of those years out in Hollywood." He turns his angry gaze on Margaret while Birdy looks helplessly from one to the other before leaving the room in a stricken huff. After a painful, silent moment, Margaret follows her into the kitchen, having no idea what to say to Cornell who is staring out the window, his face suddenly an alarming shade of pink.

Birdy is flustered and profusely apologetic, the lunch having been grievously spoiled. Margaret leaves almost immediately, her salad half-eaten, one she had been enjoying before Cornell entered into his Mr. Hyde episode. Her old schoolmate is almost in tears when Margaret says good-bye at the front door, Cornell not surfacing to make some final dig. Birdy tries to return the box of chocolates and the flowers, saying Margaret shouldn't have spent good money on a lunch ruined by a lunatic, but Margaret insists that she keep the gifts, horrified that Birdy would consider herself unworthy of a gesture so last-minute and commonplace—she wishes now that she had done something more exceptional, knowing Birdy is humiliated and will possibly suffer the shame of this encounter for months.

Birdy walks with her to the street, embracing her awkwardly. Margaret says good-bye, worrying suddenly that she will laugh at the strangeness of the day, but Birdy gives her a deeply unhappy look, saying, "I'll see you again, sometime."

Margaret nods, trying to smile. "Yes, I'll see you again. Maybe in California if you're ever out that way."

Cornell does not come outside or appear at the front windows to stare grimly at her, nor does he wave good-bye, belatedly remorseful for his unaccountable rudeness. But then, an hour and a half later, he appears at the airport, waiting for her near the check-in counter. Only two airlines offer flights to Richfield—the airport is so small that he must have known he would find her.

Seeing him there, still in his Sunday best, she feels dread. She knows that he won't attack her, but she does not want to talk to him, does not want to hear his excuses or further cynical and withering comments. He is jealous of her, simply and viciously, and she has nothing to say to him. This jealousy is nothing new; she is jealous of some people, and other people are jealous of her. It is unfortunate, sometimes corrosive, but inescapable. She has no desire to soothe him either, to tell him that it's not too late if he wants to change his circumstances—to travel, to take up his trombone again, to make a famous name for himself. This is Birdy's job, not hers.

She tightens her grip on the strap of her garment bag. He stands several yards away, waiting for her to draw closer before he takes a few steps to meet her. His expression is contrite, very tired, and she sees a blotchy stain on the front of his pale green linen shirt—salad dressing, she thinks, and feels her heart turn a little in sympathy. It is ridiculous how soft she is, something Oliver teases her about, not so gently.

Cornell reaches toward her. "Can I carry your bag?"

She shakes her head. "No, I'm fine."

He stares at her, tense and uncertain. She wishes she were on the plane already, thirty thousand feet above this scene, that it had never happened anywhere but in her head. But he is there, this good-looking, discontented man who twenty years ago had claimed a little of her imagination from time to time, nothing too personal, only that he was appealing but she had never had a real crush on him. Perhaps this was what he had hoped for at lunch? for her to say she had wanted to date him but had never had the guts to ask him out? She wouldn't have said this in front of his wife, if it had even been true.

"You might be wondering what happened back at the house," he says. "I'm very sorry about that."

"You upset Birdy."

"Yes, and you too, I think."

She says nothing. She really does not want to fall back into her ridiculed adolescent role of trying to put everyone at ease, which was rarely successful. She has power over him, and he knows it. But this power does not really interest her. She only wants to be gone, back to San Jose and her work, to her lover and his sons, to the new car she bought a week before the reunion, an expensive, frivolous foreign beauty, the first of her life.

"Listen, Margaret," he says haltingly. "I'll be honest with you. Birdy and I had a fight just before you arrived and it threw everything off-kilter."

She waits, still unwilling to help him.

"She was hoping we could befriend you, bring you back to us in some way so that you would want to keep seeing us. She wants to visit you in California and be invited into your life. She thought you'd actually be interested in this, but I knew that you wouldn't be."

She looks at him steadily. "Why did you think I wouldn't be?"

He smiles, not unkindly. "I'm a realist, Margaret. Birdy isn't."

"Were you mad," she says, her eyes on his, "because it seemed like what you had to offer her wasn't enough?"

"I don't know if I'd say that."

"No, probably you wouldn't."

"No," he says, shifting his weight from one leg to the other. "I guess not." People drift by, wheeling their luggage, talking into cell phones, some looking curiously at her and Cornell before passing them. She almost doesn't mind now that he has come to her, offered his apology and explanation. She will be able to dismiss the unease that she could imagine plaguing her back in California and can instead assign blame where it is due—not to herself, which at first was what she had feared—had the cheap chocolates offended him? the day-old grocery-store flowers? Still, it was ridiculous to believe that *she* had affronted him; she had done nothing but accept his invitation, arrived at the appointed hour, bearing gifts, inexpensive ones but gifts nonetheless. His outburst is no longer a distressing mystery; it really is only jealousy, evidence of a competitive man's insecurity.

Almost downcast, Cornell shakes her hand at the counter where she needs to pick up her boarding pass. He tells her again how sorry he is and then he is gone.

On the plane she can't keep herself from brooding over him and Birdy. She wonders what Birdy's life is like, how often Cornell becomes aggressive and cruel, pouncing on people so unexpectedly. She wonders if possibly he is manic-depressive—his enthusiasm and sweetness in the parking lot the previous night in direct opposition to today's performance. Perhaps he met Birdy when he was in the hospital after some catastrophic episode, she falling for his good looks and charm, knowing what a disaster he would be, but thinking that she could help him. Margaret knows plenty of other couples who began with this same premise, most of them as successful as a stiltwalker in an earthquake.

No, it is probably nothing like this. Cornell is unextraordinary—not mentally disturbed, just bored sometimes and dissatisfied with Richfield, with his life and its outcomes so far. He is a character she knows well, the one who is often her hero, or else, her anti-hero. Often they are the same person.

She doesn't mention the abortive lunch to Oliver until the following day, bringing it up almost idly, telling him as she puts breakfast dishes in his dishwasher that the Schweitzers were unfit hosts, the lunch ending with the wife crying and the husband sitting alone at the dining room table, angrily chewing his food. Then his unexpected arrival at the airport, the self-rescue from disgrace.

Oliver sets down his newspaper, his graying hair still rumpled from sleep. She smiles, self-conscious as he looks at her for a long second before replying. "Sounds like it was staged for your benefit. They're probably hoping you'll write about them."

She shakes her head. "He can't be that good of an actor."

"How would you know? You haven't seen him in twenty years."

"I really doubt it, Oliver. Birdy was truly distressed."

"Maybe she didn't know what he was up to."

"Maybe," she says, doubtful.

"Call them. See what they say about it now."

"No. I don't want to revisit any part of it."

He tilts his head, shrugging minutely. "Then I suppose it will forever remain a mystery. Don't feel bad about it. Some people are very odd. You know that as well as anyone."

"Are you glad the lunch was a disaster? You didn't want me to go in the first place."

He shakes his head. "No, I'm not. I just wish I had been there to put that jerk in his place."

Her work does not go well when she returns to it. The screenplay she is adapting from the violent, bewildering novel is a cheerless grind when she sends it to the producer a week after Richfield. He tosses it back at her for revision almost instantly, with a memo that begins, *"It's a piece of shit, Maggie. Don't castrate the son of a bitch. Leave in the two rape sequences. Don't cut out the scene where the teacher gets his fingers chopped off by the psychotic student in the middle of the night. This book has balls. You've turned it into a bedtime story for pre-adolescents . . ."* His profane tirade goes on for a page and a half, leaving her with the urge to descend on his cavernous office and chop off *his* fat, greasy fingers. The trip to Richfield has upset her equilibrium, leaving her unable to concentrate for hours at a time as she had once done without strain, as if she were riding a bike down a hillside, coasting all the way to the bottom. The screenplay is punishment for her complacency, for her faith in her talents—a faith she hasn't had seriously challenged since before her second film's success, seven years ago now. She has grown accustomed to hearing her name spoken with respect— her follow-through, her quality work a given.

Several times she has nearly done what Oliver suggested so flippantly; she has almost called the Schweitzers' house to check on them, Birdy in particular, but she does not want to make this gesture that Cornell might think a triumph—he has succeeded in reaching through the depths of so much time and distance, their lives colliding with hers, leaving their jagged impression when initially they might have thought her unassailable.

As she works through the revision, hating all of the ugliness, the ugly characters, knowing she doesn't want to do another project like this one, no matter how big the paycheck, she receives a letter from Richfield, sent to her post office box, the same address the reunion committee used for all of their peppy, hopeful correspondence.

25 August

Dear Margaret,

I hope you will accept my apology for any discomfort we may have caused you on the day you came to lunch. I know it must also have been awkward for you to have Cornell chase you to the airport, but I couldn't stop him. I felt like such a fool and still do. You probably hate us now and think we're very strange. But I promise you we're not. Really, we're not. It's just that a person like you doesn't show up in Richfield every day and I guess we got a little excited. I really hope that we'll have a chance to meet again under happier circumstances. I'm so sorry about all of the awkwardness and bad feelings we probably caused you. If you ever think of us, please know that we admire you and your work very much.

My very best wishes,
Birdy Schweitzer

She doesn't reproach Birdy for wanting to become a part of her life; the desire to make a new friend is nothing if not a wish to better oneself. She is reminded of her own hunger before her first successes, when she craved attention and recognition from acquaintances who had already made a name for themselves. Like Birdy, she wanted to meet people who would change her life. She has always yearned for romantic gestures, has always wanted to inspire them and knows she now sometimes does, in the thousands who see her movies and return home to a life subtly altered by what they have experienced in the darkened theater, even if in most cases it is only for a few days. She has worked for years for this, to be a stranger benignly affecting another, traveling across the invisible boundaries of time and circumstance.

But Cornell, she cannot know what he thinks of her or her work anymore. He is only one man, so far removed from the industry as to be an absurdity. He shouldn't matter to her one bit, but he does. Almost a month has passed since the reunion, but she is still upset that he resented her so much that day. She suspects he will now look only for the faults in her films, allowing them to ruin any pleasure he could feel instead. He is cheating himself, though she is a party to this shortchange, unwilling but nonetheless involved, as if by hastily turning a corner, she has caused two drivers to collide. There is no way ever to know what has possibly been done in her name—a torment and a mercy, this ability to remain ignorant of any blame assigned by strangers. How lucky she thought herself at one time, knowing there were countless ways to be a part of someone else's life: this surely the one human enterprise that eclipses all others, its authority so stunning, almost terrifying.

By the Way

And what, in the hidden, velvet-lined chambers of his heart, do I think he holds most dear? There must be, fixed but quivering, a boyhood coonskin cap, an Alaskan cruise taken at age fourteen, a championship Pac-man score and several issues of *Mad Magazine,* a large serving of truly celestial lasagna, a half-dozen Bruce Springsteen songs, and maybe, if I'm really lucky, the picture he took of my hand holding a sweating lemonade glass. It could be worse, I know. It could be taxidermied armadillos and Foghat lyrics and velvet Elvis portraits and a brand new can of honey-roasted peanuts and the one time he got to lower the flag in the third grade. Though I suppose that's not so bad. It's not like he's squeezing kittens until they pop or burning all of his baby pictures while his mother weeps on the other side of the bathroom door because he thinks he looks like a skinned otter.

The thing is, he's thirty-seven and at fifty-five, it's obvious I'm nowhere close, which also means, supposedly, that I'm on the downward slope. I've reached the unfortunate landmark where I'm now eligible for AARP membership (but who, other than the fabled one percent of the richest among us, is able to retire at fifty-goddamn-five?) Miles doesn't know my age, in any case. He thinks I'm somewhere around forty-three which I decided to let him believe when we began talking about age differences on the third date. Apparently I'm the first older woman he's dated since he was fifteen. Some would say we're a match taken straight from a circus sideshow. Others would say I'm a dirty old woman. What I say is that I can, at least for the moment, and so I do.

Something not everyone seems to realize is that the worst thing about getting older is that so many people will always be younger than you. Much, much younger. And the world's industrious babymakers keep pumping out more and more children each year to ensure that those of us firmly mired in middle age don't forget we're inching ever closer to the date of our expiration. At thirty-seven, Miles is still so painfully young that I have to keep myself from turning weepy whenever I see his unlined face after a day or two apart or if I let myself think too long about the gap between us—not to mention what will most likely happen when he finds out how wide it in fact is.

Because of course the chilling truth is that I could be his mother. And his ten-year-old son's grandmother. Patrick lives with Miles's ex-wife Faye, a law-school girlfriend he helped get pregnant in their last year at John Marshall and subsequently married before divorcing five years later. Patrick and Faye live on the south side of the city, near the big university hospital where Faye is a member of the legal staff, and Miles lives on the north side, four blocks from my apartment which we haven't spent much time in because, among other things, I'm afraid he'll be scared off by the sorry state of my brain these days.

The thing is, I think I might be dying. Not in the one-day-at-a-time slow-motion way that healthy people are dying, instead how the terminally ill are taken down—the body under siege, an authentic corporeal blitzkrieg that wipes its victims out without remorse. Early Alzheimer's. Its name is an ice pick splintering off bits of my hardening brain. Yesterday I forgot to pick up Rosie, my yellow Lab, from the groomer's. They had to call me a half an hour before closing to remind me that the poor dog had been waiting since eleven for her mistress to show some mercy. A few days before this, I left forty dollars' worth of groceries in the trunk of my car overnight. I had gone out after work to fill my aging Toyota with gas and to buy some milk and a few other things, but by the time I got home, I had forgotten that I'd made the trip to the Jewel, so the frozen vegetables, the gallon of 1%, the cheese and turkey slices were ruined when I finally remembered the next morning. On top of this recent disaster, I miss close friends' birthdays increasingly often; I forget to take my vitamins or write out the checks for the phone and electric bills or return library books. That is, unless I remember to write myself notes to do these things. My apartment has become a leafy forest of green and yellow Post-it notes.

Leslie, my ex-husband, is the only man I've allowed to see the physical evidence of my brain's increasing disarray. The few times Miles has been over, I've cleaned everything up, taken down the pastel Post-it quilt that covers my refrigerator, along with most of the notes on the three cork-boards I've lately installed to help me keep my thoughts from scattering even further. Leslie has his own theory about this scary new idiosyncrasy of mine. In general, he has many theories, being something of a know-it-all; he also is a note-writer, so he feels some sympathy for me, though he thinks for the most part that I'm imagining my troubles, holding open the door for them by allowing the Post-it count throughout my house to escalate. The last time he stopped by, he added to the exquisite corpse of my neurosis or whatever the hell it is, by taping a scrap of green paper to the bathroom door that read: *Dearest X* (his silly nickname for me), *Go to the goddamn doctor if you think you're going crazy. Why will your supposed condition into being by your obsessive worrying? Aren't you supposed to be spending your free time babysitting Miles? (Sorry, I couldn't resist. As the guy who domesticated you all those years ago, you have to allow me that). Still yours, L. P.S. You remember who I am, don't you? Who Miles is? . . . just checking.*

Honestly, I know this is all a bit alarmist. I can still do both of my jobs perfectly well, but it's not the kind of work that requires me to keep track of a thousand different details or a hundred clients' whims. I wouldn't have the goods to be something like a waitress or a doctor or an accountant. I teach dance classes part-time with Leslie at an overpriced dance studio on Southport, and another twenty hours a week I edit college textbooks at home; for the most part, all I'm expected to do is take care of the punctuation, grammar and syntax—not the integrity of the facts and formulas, which they have a peer editor for.

I'm in the middle of a chapter about the American bank panic and great depression of the 1890s when the doorbell rings. It's four o'clock in the afternoon on a Thursday and I'm expecting precisely no one. That is, if I remember correctly, which for once, I think I actually do. I suspect it's Leslie, wanting to talk about his retirement portfolio which is much more well-endowed than my own, and he likes to rub it in. One little way to avenge himself for Miles, probably. Leslie is dating no one he's nuts about right now, though he is dating, having his usual share of offers from pretty, lonely women at the dance studio, and unlike me, he rarely bothers to answer to his conscience when it comes to accepting what they offer.

On my way to the door, the cloudy hallway mirror informs me that I look tired, even a little haggard, and my eyebrows, for some reason, look crooked, though I had them threaded by a talented cosmetician in her bustling and fragrant beauty parlor a few days ago, and up until now, they looked perfect. Depressed, I yell an irritated hello into the intercom.

"Hey Sasha, it's me!" pipes a voice I can now recognize after the first syllable.

His enthusiasm is adorable but I feel about a hundred and twenty percent panic-stricken. The apartment is a colossal mess, Post-Its everywhere (*Take Rosie for walk at 6 p.m.!! Take B-vitamins at 4 p.m.!,* ad infinitum), my hair a rat's nest, the post-lunch lipstick long-since chewed off.

"Hello?" he repeats, tentative. "Are you still there?"

"Yes," I finally choke out. "I'm here."

"Can you buzz me up?"

"Miles, well, maybe I should come down?"

He pauses. "Why? Is someone up there with you?"

"No, I'm alone. I'm working, that's all."

"Oh," he says, his voice very small. "Should I come back later?"

"No, no, it's fine. You can come on up. But give me a couple of minutes to pick up a few things. The place looks like a bomb site." I buzz him in but don't yet unlock my door. He has several flights ahead of him; the elevator has been on the fritz for four days now, my neighbors and I forced to use the freight elevator by the back entrance, but I haven't told Miles about it because he hasn't been here since old unfaithful broke down.

Heart thundering, my nose suddenly, despicably, dripping, and I'm tearing Post-its by the handful from the walls on my way down the hall, realizing that I'll have to risk leaving most of them up because otherwise I won't have enough time left over to do something about my face. The news is bad by the bathroom lights too: dark circles, a wrinkled forehead, birds' feet marching out from the corners of my eyes. These unfortunates are called the fruits of wisdom by the insane optimists, but I would rather go hungry. I slap on some toner and a light coat of ivory base, take a pencil to my eyebrows, put on fresh lipstick and finish with a few strokes of mascara. All of this takes two and a half minutes. After forty years of playing seriously with cosmetics, I could apply them in the midnight dark.

Miles knocks, the sound almost shy, and somehow I remember to make sure my armpits are ready for visitors. I've never kept a curtain there, even during college when I once let my leg hair grow for months, after reading Betty Friedan and Gloria Steinem and deciding that men needed to shave off the signs of their animal selves too if women were expected to. I was half-assed about feminism, too much of a priss to make any kind of real statement. The fact is, I liked my smooth skin, I liked the gleam of freshly shaved knees. Needless to say, I didn't last long as a Friedan acolyte.

The second I open the door, my much-younger man lunges forward and kisses me. It's this completely unselfconscious exuberance that I think I love most about him. And he's also the only man I've ever slept with who has admitted to the most singularly charming quirks that I have ever heard: he once meant to make a career of planting marigolds for old ladies with back troubles; he used to save the tufts of hair that Angus, his childhood collie, shed with the intention of using them to make a pillow for his mother; he has held onto his grandmother's collection of pressed flowers because he wants to frame them for his daughter's room if he ever has a daughter. This boy is a romantic, no question. He fell for me, I guess, because I know how to dance, and he's wildly jealous of Les but won't admit it. I can't exactly blame him either because my ex and I know exactly what we're doing when we're on the floor, showing our students how to move together in such a lithe and splendid way that we are in fact making a kind of kinetic-poetic love. Miles was one of our students for two weeks; he dropped out during the third week because he said he had to ask me out once he found out that Les and I weren't an item, and he didn't know if I would consider dating a student, even if the dance studio is a far cry from any college's seriousness. Still, I don't generally go out with students, but for him I would definitely have made an exception. Miles is a tall man with long-fingered hands. . . I leave the rest to the dirty

He is possibly the most beautiful man-child of any I have ever been lucky enough to take into my bed. I can't tell him what a liar I am because I'm fairly sure that I'm in love with him. It's fucking awful.

(While sleeping, Les's face looked a little like Gary Cooper's; during sex, he looked like Peter Lorre—wildly disorienting to have him hovering above me with that frightening, bug-eyed leer. Maybe this is ultimately why we broke up. Miles looks like Harrison Ford. At all times. Sometimes I don't know if I'll be able to keep from proposing marriage or else taking him hostage.)

He doesn't unearth himself from my bed until well past seven o'clock and I want to cry when he goes. I confessed nothing about my brain or my age. His smell is on my pillows and I bury my face in them, feeling like an old fool, a stricken Bette Davis who must have known it when her brain began to go to seed. At least the list of those who have gone before me into the cerebral nether regions is illustrious. Even so, this isn't a particularly comforting thought.

No more than thirty minutes after my poor, duped lover leaves, the doorbell rings again. This time it's Leslie and I really have no desire whatsoever. But he insists on coming up, despite the weary warning in my voice. The man has almost never had any room for *no* in his vocabulary and within seconds, I can hear him bounding up the stairs, two at a time, very healthy and vain about it in his still-young-old-age.

"Don't you remember that we made plans for dinner tonight?" he says, looking a little hurt.

Of course I don't remember. And this just wrecks me. I stare at him for several seconds, so upset by this—yet another hint that I really have gone round the bend. "I don't remember anything anymore," I finally say, "which is something *you* seem to have forgotten."

He cracks a devious smile. "I'm just teasing you, sweetie. We didn't have plans, so don't worry. But as long as you persist in believing that you're losing your mind, I'm going to give you a hard time about it. Just go to the damn doctor and he'll say the same thing I'm saying—it's all in your head. No pun intended," he laughed. "Anyway, I just thought I'd drop by to see if you felt like ducking out for a little dinner."

I pretend to take a swing at him and feel my face spasm with the desire to sob. He nimbly steps away and does a little spin, this would-be Fred

minds of the world. One other thing: his deep and beautiful voice. Perfect for phone sex, something I figured out a few nights ago when he couldn't come over, his son innocently asleep on the other side of his prurient father's apartment.

"I really wanted to see you," he says when we pry our lips apart. "I got out early because we had to evacuate the floor after a janitor accidentally spilled some kind of bleach mixture down the hall and the stench invaded all of the offices. I know I probably should have called but I thought I'd try for a sneak attack."

"That's very thoughtful of you," I say, trying to suppress a smile. "The attack was a success. I definitely didn't see it coming."

"Should I let you get back to your work? I'm sorry I didn't call first."

"Don't be silly. I was about to take a break anyway."

"You've told me that you like surprises," he says, abashed. "Unless you weren't serious."

I tangle my fingers in his dark hair. It is as soft as kitten fur. I want to press my nose to it, smell his piney man-shampoo but make myself wait. I'm pretty sure that he's come here to be pawed at, that soon we'll stop being coy. "I do like surprises. Some are just a little more surprising than others. But you're the kind of surprise I'd like more of."

He follows me into the kitchen where I pour us each a glass of mineral water and ignore his third and fourth apologies. For someone who's supposed to be quite a success in the courtroom, he is endearingly unsure of himself when it comes to our fledgling relationship. I'm not much better off, but I'm pretty sure he doesn't know this.

We sit with thighs touching on the worn leather sofa in the living room, Rosie snuffling around our feet, Miles her new favorite friend, something that would also make Leslie jealous if I were mean enough to tell him. Les is my ex because after twenty years of living and working together, I suppose the truth is we grew tired of seeing so much of each other. There were no children to keep up appearances for either. We stopped having sex, and both of us ended up getting involved with other people about whom we used to have the most painfully civil conversations until we realized it was less uncomfortable to say nothing. Whatever passion we had left for each other seemed only to manifest itself at the dance studio; after another year of limping along, he moved out of our apartment and

I stayed put. This was seven years ago. Since then I've had five boyfriends, quasi- and more authentic, but no one near as silly, adorable and whip-smart as Miles.

"Are you hungry?" I ask, thinking I could give him some of the vegetable soup I made last night. Les is right, in a way, when he talks about me babysitting my new boyfriend. I do want to take care of him and wonder sometimes how he's able to take care of a son of his own, how he handles all of his lawyerly responsibilities, how he gets away with such an unruly hairdo at work.

He shakes his scruffy head and glances at the pile of books on the coffee table. On top are five-pound picture books about Martha Graham, the Joffrey and the Bolshoi ballets. "How long was it that you danced with that company in New York?" he says between sips of water. "I have a hard time believing you weren't the star."

"Keep dreaming, cutie. I barely even got to dance a solo. I only lasted two and a half years before my knees started to give me a lot of trouble."

"You couldn't do some physical therapy and get back into it?"

"I tried, but it didn't work out. I'd lost confidence and couldn't do the leaps without worrying about tearing a tendon. When that starts to happen, it's basically over for most ballet dancers."

After a moment he says, "You'd met Les by then anyway and off you went to Chicago."

"Yes, basically." Miles does not know how long Les and I were together. He thinks it was somewhere around eleven years, not twenty-two. I know I have to tell him the truth, probably very soon, or else he's going to dump me so fast when he figures it out that he'll likely break the sound barrier. But I have no idea how to begin, how to tell the one man in the world I least want to disappoint that I am potentially the biggest disappointment he's ever encountered.

And on top of that, my brain is turning into the cerebral equivalent of a moth-eaten quilt.

He's not a fool, however. Certainly his livelihood depends on him not being one. He knows something's going on in the decaying back of my mind and gives me an appraising look. "What's the real reason you didn't want me to come up here?"

I look at him, my lips twitching. "I was cooking some meth. Don't you realize that I could blow up the whole building if I'm not careful?"

He laughs, squeezing my knee. "I was wondering what that fur smell was. I didn't want to say anything, but now I know."

I stare at him, horrified. "Does it really smell in here? I took out t garbage this morning but I don't think it smelled bad before I did." I sni a few times, my face turning a furious pink. "Do you really smell som thing?" It's hard not to wonder, my armpits already prickling with ne vous sweat, if this is another one of my brain's increasingly dirty tricks I've read that some people with brain tumors sometimes can't swallow or keep their balance or they forget family members' names and faces, and it's probable that one's sense of smell could also be obliterated. I'm starting to get used to the idea of Alzheimer's, but a tumor is not . . .well, I don't know if I'm at all ready to consider this sort of alien invader.

Miles is making a clownish face, his eyes bugged, his eyebrows arched like the Joker's. "I'm kidding," he cries. "Don't worry. It smells like jasmine or carnations in here. Something very flowery."

"It's lavender and rose potpourri." I exhale some of the anxious air in my lungs.

He's still looking at me, now a little uncertain. "What's going on with you?" he asks quietly. "You really do seem distracted."

"The place is a mess," I say. "I don't usually have so many Post-its up. You must think I'm a bit of a wacko."

He shakes his head. "Don't be silly. How else would you keep track of all of the details for the books you're working on?"

"I'm only working on one book right now. Most of those Post-its aren't for it."

"I don't care what they're for. You're the most together person I've met in a long time."

He must have been smoking something very potent from Mexico on the way home from work, but I don't say a word. What I'm thinking of doing is confessing my fears about my fragmenting brain because with one of the two big secrets I've been keeping from him out in the open, I might not feel so bad about letting him continue to think I'm too young to be his son's grandmother. But before I can open my mouth, he's kissing me and I don't want to stop him from undressing me for something like the fifteenth time since we've started taking off each other's clothes. I lov his furry chest, his strong, callused hands; all of the delicate cells of h beautiful male body with its tiny, hard butt and bony knees and big fee

Astaire with his pretty steel-gray curls and feather-weight feet. ("If only I knew the right person to get us an in out in Hollywood," he used to say when we were first married. "We could take our rightful place next to Fred and Ginger." Frankly, I would rather have taken my rightful place next to Mikhail Baryshnikov, but I never told Leslie this. The closest I ever got to the great Misha was when we exchanged hellos and a couple of meaningful glances [his eyebrows raised with a smile, my face turning savagely hot in an instant] at an Upper East Side party where he was ringed by ten other hungry women who all wore leotards and murderous shoes to work too. Nevertheless, I lasted quite a while on that one moment; years, in truth.)

"Your little friend was here, wasn't he," says Leslie. "I can smell him on you."

"No, you can't," I say, half-embarrassed, half-defiant.

"But he was here, right?"

"That's none of your business."

"Don't get bent out of shape. You deserve as many good times in the sack as the next person."

I don't bother with a retort.

"I'm just saying," he murmurs.

We end up ordering Thai from a place a few blocks away, Leslie running back down the stairs to pick up the spicy rice noodles and spring rolls while I get in the shower and reluctantly rinse off Miles's scent before toweling off and slipping on my robe. I don't care how I look in front of my ex when we aren't working. I have no idea if I'll ever feel this comfortable with Miles if I don't lose my mind first or he dumps me when he finds out my real age. As I see it, I have about five to ten, maybe fifteen, more years of being a striking woman. After that, I suppose it'll be time for the chin straps and face-lifts and a strict avoidance of the sun which I'll probably have to cry over because I love my beach vacations and have never taken shelter under palm trees or big umbrellas, just a straw hat, and sporadically at best. My mother's Italian mother shared with me her olive skin and dark hair that's going gray slowly, just one strand at a time—it's a fight to the death and so far the brown is winning.

"How serious are you about this young guy?" asks Leslie, his mouth half-full but I stop myself from telling him to finish chewing before he talks. I hate being a scold, which is another reason why our marriage didn't last.

"Why are you so interested? Are you afraid I'll replace you with him?"

"You already have," he snorts. "I'm not sleeping in your bed anymore, am I?"

"You wouldn't want to be."

"That's not strictly true."

I shake my head. "Don't even pretend you still have regrets. What's the point?"

"I just like teasing you."

"I know. It's is the one thing that's never gotten old for you when it comes to me."

He smiles and shakes his head. Sometimes I wonder why we're still friends. Lately, more often than not, I want to clobber him. I suppose my annoyance is due in part to the fact that for the first time since our divorce, I'm genuinely in love with another man and it's not at all easy, though I doubt it ever really is.

"Can I stay and watch some TV for a little while?" he asks when we're washing the dinner plates.

"I don't think it's a good idea tonight."

"What, you've got work to do? That's all right. You do your work, and I'll happily sit by myself on the couch and be a deadbeat for an hour or two."

"What's wrong with your TV?"

"Nothing, it's a thing of beauty, but it's at my house, not yours."

To avoid a stupid argument, I tell him he can stay for an hour if he really has to, and he decides to celebrate by helping himself to the last bottle of Belgian beer in the refrigerator. I go down the hall, sit at my desk and stare at the text that I abandoned hours ago, the 1890s bank panic much less interesting than it was before Miles rang the doorbell and waltzed his lovely way into the disorder of my home and heart. No more than five minutes later, the phone rings and it's him, his voice giving me goosebumps because I feel as if I conjured his call out of the ether. I can barely speak I'm so pleased. He asks permission to come over again and maybe spend the night? because he's found that he's having trouble getting any work done. "The thing is," he says very quietly, "I keep picturing you naked. I've tried everything to stop, but for some reason, I just can't do it. I hope this doesn't happen in court on Friday, otherwise the judge will probably have to put me in his chambers and bring me a cold compress."

There are few things that I can imagine enjoying hearing more than this, especially delivered in the deep voice of this shy young lawyer with two left feet, but what I say next is perhaps the most boneheaded thing I've said since the ninth grade when I hinted to my algebra teacher that from the side view, her butt looked like a couch cushion.

"I'd love for you to come over, but Leslie's here and I took a shower and need to get myself dressed again, so give me about a half an hour or so to tidy up and kick him out?"

There is a long, long pause. Mountains could be razed and reborn in that pause; the human race could die out and the earth repopulated with bison and great horned owls. "Oh," he says in a tight little voice. "It sounds like you're busy. Maybe some other time then."

"No," I almost shout. "You can come over tonight. Leslie wasn't supposed to be here. He showed up a little while ago and I had just taken a shower and he wanted to have dinner and now he's watching TV and I'm trying to get some work done."

"Sasha, if you and Leslie had plans tonight, that's okay with me. You don't have to explain yourself."

"I know it must sound a little strange, but it really isn't. Please come over."

"No, I don't think I should. You're busy. Another time."

I want to keep pleading with him but I suspect that Leslie can hear me and I also know that no matter what I say, Miles will not come over. In the few seconds it took to make my asinine utterance, something mighty shifted in him, something that possibly won't shift back, and I realize then that he has felt from the start that I have had all of the clout in our involvement, that he has been pursuing me like an adoring groupie. It also seems possible that he could be as taken with me as I am with him.

No matter the futility, I have to try one more time. "Please come over. I want to see you too."

"Another time, Sasha."

We hang up after his morose and my nearly tearful goodbye, and it's clear that I will have to go to him immediately. I will have to tell him the secrets I've been keeping these past weeks and cry on his soon-to-be rigid shoulder and beg for his indulgence, if not his love and acceptance.

Leslie has his shoes on and is almost at the door when I emerge from my office with the cargo of my hangdog face and frantically beating heart.

"Trouble in paradise?" he says, managing to look a little sorry.

"I have to go out."

"I can tell. I'll see you tomorrow night then. The rumba and the swing are on the bill."

"I haven't forgotten."

"Just making sure," he winks, unable to resist this little dig.

I slam the door behind him but don't really mean it. I'm too tired and depressed to keep my dander up for more than a few seconds. It takes me almost forty minutes to put myself in some kind of shape for the break-up that I'm about to walk into, four blocks and five flights down from where my wretched self currently mopes. Miles might have gone out and decided to pick up some much younger woman in a bar instead of sit at home and keep drawing the very wrong and ugly conclusion that Leslie and I are still sleeping together. He's seen us dance, so of course he thinks so. I would too if I were him.

But that's the least of my troubles. The worst thing will be telling him that he's been dating a woman who's nowhere close to living in the province of forty-three. It hardly seems like it now, but the truth is, I used to be so tough and smart and proud of myself. I don't know what has happened over the past ten years that has transformed me into such a wreck, except for the new wrinkles that appear almost weekly now and the endless parade of young, beautiful actresses and pop stars and news anchors who seem to get more indestructible as each year passes—scientists will have figured out a way to keep these dolls' faces from showing their age by the time they reach forty, but for the rest of us, it's much too late. Age is grief and few of us know how to defy it; the curse is this—we see ourselves and others in years, not good deeds or brilliant work.

So I'm stuck with a web of lies of my own weaving, and I'm really smitten and very sad. Oh, and I almost forgot—I'm also losing my mind.

Miles answers his bell after I've pressed it twice; he sounds surprised but not at all hostile when he hears my voice. Even so, by the time I climb the two flights to his doorstep, my stomach has dropped to my ankles. He hasn't yet opened the door. Like a stranger, I have to knock and it's several more seconds before he bothers to open it. His face is carefully arranged when he lets me in, an I'm-not-the-least-bit-upset-or-jealous look sitting precariously on top of what's really cooking: You'd-better-make-this-good-otherwise-we're-through. I reach out to hug him and he lets me, but when I try to melt into him, breasts pressing into his chest, midriff smothering the edge of his privates, he squirms away, knowing that he can't think clearly in my embrace. "Do you want something to drink?" he asks, his eyes meeting mine before darting away.

"Sure, whatever you're having is fine."

"Sparkling water," he says. "I've been trying to read over my case notes."

"I'll take some."

He comes back with two glasses of tap water instead, explaining that the Pellegrino's gone flat. We sit on the couch, distinctly not touching, mired in awkwardness and failing confidence. He asks when the book I'm editing needs to be completed. I ask if he's worried about the court date on Friday—anything to avoid the real business we need to attend to. I can't just blurt out that I know he's jealous of Leslie but has no reason to be. Unpleasant as it is for me to admit it, we aren't yet comfortable enough with each other for me to say that I'm aware of his insecurities and have possibly figured out a way to take the thorns out of them.

We sip the tap water, not sure what to do with our hands, until someone in the vast world that mutely surrounds us shows a little mercy—his phone rings. He gets up to answer it in the kitchen and makes me wait for almost ten minutes. It doesn't take me to long to figure out that it's his ex-wife, trying to get him to commit to taking their son for the next three weekends. My heart sinks as I eavesdrop, wondering how he's found space for me in his crowded life. I know that the fact he so far has means that he's really wanted to and that before tonight we were probably on our way to something he hoped would become a feature of the very busy life of Miles Frederick Jantsen, resident wunderkind at Stroud, Pierce and Wyatt.

"Sorry about that," he says, finally returning to the couch. "She's already called twice tonight. I didn't want to answer but I knew she'd keep calling back."

I nod, open my mouth and blurt out one of the nasty things that has been crouching in the pit of my stomach for weeks. "I'm not forty-three."

He blinks. "Okay."

I hesitate, unable to hold his gaze. "I think maybe you've thought that I am."

"No, I haven't thought that," he says quietly. "At first, yes, but I stopped thinking it pretty quickly."

I don't know if I should be offended or relieved, but the latter more or less wins out. Advancing decrepitude has made me sanguine, I guess. Or else just resigned. "How old do you think I am?"

"You want the truth?" he asks.

I nod.

"You don't look it, but I know you're somewhere around fifty."

"How long have you known this?"

"About as long as we've been seeing each other. You might have heard that there's a little thing out there called the World Wide Web. I looked you up not long after the first class I took with you and Leslie and found some pictures of you dancing in New York in the mid-seventies. It's pretty hard to hide the facts of your life from anyone, Sasha, especially if you've ever been a public figure."

"I was hardly a public figure."

"You were gorgeous in those pictures. You still are."

I can't look at him. "Hardly," I mumble.

"I don't agree." He has inched closer, placed one hand tentatively on my thigh. I can smell his rainy, cut-grass scent and suspect with almost tearful relief that I'm probably not going to be tossed out the door and into the indifferent night.

"I don't know how much more time I have of being pretty. Not much, I'd bet. I think I'm losing my mind too. I have trouble remembering things that shouldn't be a problem." I tell him about Rosie and the groomers, about the groceries, about the ever-lengthening Post-it quilts, but he is not at all convinced.

"The more you worry, the worse it gets," he says. "Everyone says they're losing their memories and of course we all are, but in most cases, it's not happening as fast as we think. Slow down on the Post-its and I guarantee you'll remember just as much as you do with them, if not more."

I say that I want to believe him, but we will have to see. It's been too traumatic for me lately to dismiss all of my doubts so offhandedly. But it's a bit breathtaking to listen to him because he sounds so confident. His diagnosis is basically the same as Leslie's, but it's much more sweet coming from Miles, even if I don't feel that much better. "You don't really want to date a woman my age, do you?"

"Does it seem like I don't want to?"

". . . well, no."

"But I would like to know if Leslie is still allowed some part of you that I want only for myself."

I shake my head. "He isn't. We stopped sleeping together long before the divorce. We're just business partners now."

He studies me for a long time. "It doesn't seem like you're lying."

"I wouldn't lie to my attorney."

He can't suppress a smile. "That's a good thing. Just try to relax about your memory problems. All of the work they've piled on you lately would make anyone feel a little disoriented."

(There's also the enormous, unspoken fact that I have been trying to seem a lot younger than I am in order to keep this beautiful, improbably smitten man from walking straight through a series of doors that he won't turn around and walk back through ever again. If he's thought of this too, he has had the good manners not to voice it.

That he doesn't think I'm losing my mind is perhaps the nicest thing he could do for me. I really want to believe him because he has done two other important things in the last few minutes: 1) he hasn't dumped me, and 2) he hasn't asked me just how old I really am. In the hidden, velvet-lined chambers of my own heart the young woman I once was still holds court. She will not go her own way, and this perhaps is one of the hardest things to live with—rarely can we stop seeing ourselves as we once were. We keep savaging our own hearts when we look back and wonder what has happened to us, why we all have to suffer the hardship of losing who we once were, even as we know we're lucky to be around to grow older. We watch our faces and bodies change into something we knew was coming but still are ashamed. I loved who I once was; I do not know if I will ever love who I am becoming. Miles will love me for a while, I know, but if he will love me for the rest of my life—well, I have to doubt this. I have eighteen years on him, after all—he will be fifty-seven when I am seventy-

five, still a vigorous man, undoubtedly with much younger women pant-
ing after him if he continues to look like Harrison Ford, which most likely
he will, because Harrison himself is in his sixties and he still looks like
Harrison Ford.

Miles tells me that he wants me to stay the night. I say that I will. I have
him now and will keep him for as long as I can. This is way of all things, I
suppose. This is the one way.)

Alex Rice Inc.

She finds his name on her roster two days before the start of the fall semester and then can only stare at it. At first she doesn't want to believe it. It seems a petty joke, meant only to disorient her. But he is there with twenty other names, as rumors all summer have claimed he would be, this thirty-two-year-old movie actor, now a full-time student at the university where she has taught American literature for four years. Apparently he is intent on becoming something other than a veteran of a few expensive flops and a half-dozen vacuous blockbusters. Over the past several years, without really meaning to, she has absorbed the elemental facts of his celebrity resume: the titles of his films and the names of some of his co-stars, his two divorces, the alleged defeat of an addiction to alcohol, possibly cocaine. He owns at least one home on each coast—a Manhattan apartment, a Hollywood Hills fortress. She can only imagine what else there is, what his agent and publicist have successfully suppressed.

And now, in the limelit center of their urban campus with its thousands of first- and second-generation college students, its homesick freshmen, its bustling, already-weary faculty, sits this very handsome, very famous, blond-haired man. He has descended on her classroom with the force of his money and celebrity, the twin engines that for the past decade have propelled him headlong into public success and private failure, the naked fact of his fame a hassling second presence in her classroom. He has chosen a desk in the middle row, along the wall, his head and body stiffly upright, as if he has already transformed himself into an earnest student, one who will submit to her whims and directives each afternoon that he presents himself to her. She will have to instruct, humor, judge, and finally, grade him. This realization almost makes her snort with laughter, but the fact of him is too serious, too momentous: how to read his work without thinking, *This is the paper a movie star has written?* My god, she thinks. A goddamn movie star in my goddamn classroom.

The only other film stars she can think of who took time off to go to college are all talented women who apparently did very well at the East Coast schools where they were enrolled. Famous men, perhaps, are unwilling to risk losing their foothold in a notoriously mercurial industry. Or maybe they worry they aren't smart enough. Whatever Alex Rice's motives, she can acknowledge that he has made a brave move.

It is late August, oppressively humid, and her assigned room has no air conditioning. The class has been scheduled to meet in one of the university's oldest buildings, the open windows facing west, the afternoon sun assaulting her and the twenty-one other bodies that will be required to sit and supposedly learn together from 3:00 to 4:30 p.m. on Mondays and Wednesdays for the next fifteen weeks. She is sweating and nervous and giddily irritated. Seeing Alex Rice for the first time, she feels her face redden. He smiles at her and nods, and though she has trouble believing it, he seems a little nervous too, or else dazed.

"Hello everyone," she says, looking away from him, her voice cracking. "I assume you're all here for English 214, a course on the twentieth-century American novel." She feels a sudden, ruthless itchiness along the edge of her right breast and squeezes her arm close, trying to bury it. "If you aren't enrolled in this section, you won't be able to stay. I don't over-enroll my classes." She glances around the room but no one stirs. Squashed down, the itch passes. "All right, I'll take attendance and then we'll go over the syllabus."

When she gets to his name on the roster, he raises his hand slightly, smiling at her again. She could tease him, say that it won't take her long to remember his name, but she doesn't do it. The other students would think she is flirting. It must be what they expect, certainly what he expects. She feels herself sweating into her dress, one she had trouble choosing that morning. Staring into her closet, she had reminded herself that she was smart, smarter than he was, at least about literature. And little else in the classroom mattered, except for respect and patience, maybe sympathy too.

He is dressed in blue jeans and a stylish black linen shirt. He is suntanned and painful to behold: famous male beauty and money, two things she has never before been so close to. The other students are cowed by him too; some of the boys, she suspects, acutely aware of their own mediocrity, while most of the girls are hushed into nervous, adoring wrecks. Some of them are pretty, some plain and chubby. Among the boys, there are one or two who would have received most of the female attention if Alex Rice were not seated in the same room.

If his age is accurate, as published in the profiles she has paged through over the years in *Vanity Fair* and a few of the junkier magazines in her doctor's and dentist's offices, she is only a year older than he is. She is unmarried, self-sufficient, childless. She has been told that she is a catch, and though she has her doubts, she hopes this is true.

Rushing through the syllabus, she is too shy to add the usual corny asides about cell phones and gum-chewing and baseball hats worn backwards—her jokes seem ridiculous now, clues to just how small the scale of her life has been. Alex Rice has worked with people who are paid millions to tell jokes. The semester stretches before her, a vast potholed road of probable indignities and minor breakdowns. She knows she shouldn't care, but she does. She wants him to like her. It is inane and predictable, but she cannot pretend otherwise.

"Any questions?" she asks, looking over everyone's heads, folding her syllabus in half.

No one raises a hand. Some of the students blink at her, as if stoned. It would be a class like any other if he weren't in it. She waits another second and then says they will do introductions—one student will briefly interview another and present him or her to the rest of the class. It is an exercise that she has begun every first class of the term with since she started teaching in graduate school. She sees Alex Rice look to his left and smile at the girl who sits in the next desk, a freckled brunette with black polish on her fingernails, her hair an avalanche of frizzy curls. The girl looks down at her notebook, blushing.

Why college? Why now? she wants to ask him. What could you possibly . . . ?

When they reach him after the first half-dozen students have stammered out a few words about their business or Spanish majors and summer jobs and the dogs named Puck and Ernie that they miss at home, he says with what sounds like real contrition, "I know it's a little weird to have me here. I'm sorry about that. Just ignore me."

Several of the girls giggle. The boys look over at him, a few of them snorting in disbelief.

"I'm not sure if anyone wants to ignore you, Alex," she says, trying not to smile. "That's exactly what I try not to do as a professor. Go ahead and let your classmate introduce you, then you can introduce her to us."

"This is Alex Rice," says the girl with the black fingernails. "I'm sure you guys already know who he is. The star of *Motor Nation* and *Catastrophe*? He was born here in Chicago and played football at Lane Tech before he went out to Hollywood and started acting in movies. He doesn't read much besides scripts, so that's why he's taking this class. He might actually major in English. He wants to read books and learn how to write better. He also wants us to know that he never dated Britney Spears."

Everyone, even the few girls and boys who were pretending to be uninterested, laugh at this last remark.

She can see that her students, her class, her semester, will probably be lost to this famous, fawned-over man. If she were another kind of teacher, the trade might be worth it because for the rest of her life, she will have these few months, with all of their movie-star anecdotes, to tell to people who, in spite of themselves, will be impressed and envious, possibly sympathetic, knowing what she had to put up with.

She looks right at Alex Rice, for the first time, and says, "I wonder if Ms. Spears would say the same thing."

He smiles, showing his brilliant teeth, and says, incredibly, "Touché, Professor Royce."

So, he is not a twit. Or else this is a word he has picked up from one of his movies. Unlikely, she thinks, considering that most of them seem to have been about men with big guns surrounded by women with big breasts. "What can you tell us about your classmate?" she says.

"This is Jackie," he says. "She's nineteen, a sophomore, and she read *War and Peace* over the summer, which she said was worth it. She's probably the first person I've met who's read it."

I've read it too, she wants to say.

Instead, she says, "You'll meet a few others here who have too."

"Like you?"

She feels her face redden again. Why do I care what he thinks? she berates herself. "Yes, like me."

He puts a hand behind his head, his right arm a black wing. He is staring at her. "How many hours of your life would you say you've spent reading?"

She likes the question; it is the kind of question she has always liked. "I don't know. Probably thousands. It would be hard to keep track."

"How many books would that be?"

"Hundreds and hundreds, maybe a thousand or two."

"Wow," he says. His smile makes her scalp prickle.

The class is hushed too, their eyes on her, some curious, but a few, she imagines, pitying.

"We should move on to the next two students," she says, looking away from him but she can feel him still watching her.

He doesn't say anything more during the rest of the introductions. He has a notebook open on his desk and she notices him scribbling in it intermittently. She thinks that he must be uncomfortable in his long-sleeved shirt and blue jeans but his face doesn't shine, nor is his hair damp at the fringes like some of the other students'. She realizes suddenly that he will drop her course, disappear back into the maw of Hollywood, return to the starlets who must be calling wherever he is now living in Chicago, urging him back to civilization, to L.A. with its smog and sun, its hotel suites and in-ground pools and other people of his kind. To her annoyance, she knows that she is jealous. One hour in her life and already she feels like he owes her something—a condition, she suspects, that must not be new to him at all.

She lets the class go a little early, another one of her first-day traditions, but Alex Rice is slow to gather his notebook and pens and stash them into his leather satchel. The satchel is so new that it gleams. A few female students flutter around him, hoping he will give them an encouraging smile, but he keeps his eyes down, and after a few seconds, the girls drift away, none of them, to her disbelief, able to breach the silence with some flirtatious little compliment. She is relieved, then embarrassed by her relief. She keeps her eyes down too, but has already noticed that he dwarfs her by several inches. He has long arms and legs, thick wavy hair, and a few wrinkles—smile lines around his mouth and eyes. She gathers her papers from the desk at the front of the room and he follows as she walks toward the door, both of them silent.

The thought is there in an instant: What does he think of my figure? He is a man who brings the thought of sex immediately to mind, in part because he has been paid to simulate it in numerous movie beds. There are also his real-life lovers, all of them gorgeous, most having been paraded across the pages of countless glossy magazines, smiling for the paparazzi or the studio photographers, skilled professionals who have always made the world of ordinary people quake with jealousy and admiration.

She doesn't turn to face him in the hall because there is a tall, goateed Latino man in jeans and a red T-shirt sitting outside the classroom. He gets to his feet when she and Alex appear. His bodyguard, she thinks, taken aback.

"Professor Royce?" says Alex.

She turns and glances from him to the other man. "Yes?"

"I just wanted to let you know that I don't have that much experience writing papers. I'm not sure how good I'll be at it."

The bodyguard seems to be smiling but his eyes are on the ground.

"Most of your classmates probably haven't written many papers yet either," she says. "Don't worry too much."

He rocks back and forth on his feet a little, one hand gripping the satchel. "I took some classes at a community college in L.A. before I started acting, but it's been a long time."

"You're welcome to come to my office hours if you'd like to go over your rough drafts. There's also the writing center where you can meet with a tutor. It's free to all students."

He blinks. "Okay, thanks."

"Not like you'd need to worry about whether or not it's free," she blurts. Her eyes dart toward the bodyguard but he is facing the wall now, inspecting a patchwork of campus flyers. *Need a French tutor? Classic movie night this Friday in SAC 220—Casablanca.* His belt bristles with electronic accoutrements, and she wonders if somewhere on his body he has hidden a stun gun or a regular gun. She has no idea if this is legal. And where are the paparazzi? Surely they must know that Alex Rice is here. But no one with a camera is anywhere in evidence.

"No, it's fine," says Alex. "I just don't know how much time I'll have to see a tutor. I'm probably going to be doing some plays while I'm here."

She tries not to show her surprise. He has never seemed the type of actor who would be taken seriously in theater. "That should be fun," she says. "Just keep up with the reading and you'll be fine." She makes a move to go, wanting to flee to her office with her traitorous blushes and self-recriminations, but he takes a step closer. She can smell him now, his scent spicy and warm.

"I don't expect you to give me a break or anything, Professor Royce. I just wanted you to know what I'm up to. I'm here to work hard and get good grades the same way everyone else does."

"Of course," she says.

He glances at the bodyguard. "This is Lou. Luis really, but he doesn't mind if you call him Lou."

"Nice to meet you, Professor," he says, offering a hand.

"Likewise, Luis."

"He keeps an eye on things for me," says Alex. "But he'll stay out in the hall during class."

She could challenge him now if she had the nerve, demand to know why he is bothering with college when he has everything, absolutely everything, that most people go to college with the hope of eventually acquiring—wealth, power, fame, beautiful lovers. Knowledge is incidental; she is not such a dimwit to think that her students yearn for knowledge more than they yearn for money and glamorous sex.

"Sorry to take up your time," he says. "I know you're busy."

"No, no, it's fine."

"I'll see you on Wednesday."

"Yes, see you on Wednesday." She turns to the bodyguard. "It was nice to meet you, Luis."

"Nice to meet you too," he says before he and Alex move down the hall, a few students stopping to stare, one of the boys calling out, "Hey, you're the guy from *Sleepwalker,* right?" She sees Alex take out a pen to sign a pair of notebooks before she rushes to her office on the other side of campus, feeling strange and embarrassed and fundamentally unbalanced.

But when she gets there, her stomach sinks—two of her best students from the previous spring are waiting outside her office door. They want to talk about Saul Bellow, having read *The Adventures of Augie March* over the summer, and their excitement attenuates her emotional disarray for as long as they sit and talk with her under the gazes of Hawthorne and Edith Wharton and John Updike, her favorite New England writers, pictures of whom she has framed and hung on her office wall. The opposite wall is Chicago—Saul Bellow, Studs Terkel, Nelson Algren. A third wall is California—John Steinbeck, Joan Didion, Nathanael West. These are the people with whom she has spent most of the past several years, at least according to Peter, her most recent ex-boyfriend, who didn't think this was as much of a virtue as she did. More than once he had reminded her that these writers were not in fact her friends, despite how much she would have liked them to be. He had so often been jealous over nothing. Several times she had asked him to read the same books she was reading so that they might talk about them, but he hadn't liked her choices—no *Age of Innocence,* no *Sister Carrie,* no *Howl.* He taught philosophy and claimed to like fiction and poetry but during the year they had dated, she had almost never seen him reading a novel or a poem. She had read Nietzsche and Kierkegaard for him, which besides being difficult, had also been unsettling. Nevertheless, she had done it to please him, but then they had broken up because among other disagreements, she would not immediately put aside Eudora Welty and Flannery O'Connor to read Machiavelli and Wittgenstein. Wasn't she interested in reading the writers who had actually made a difference in the way men ruled the world? When she hadn't said yes fast enough, he had gotten angry and accused her of smallmindedness, which she had denied, adding that he was the one acting the provincial despot and maybe the world would be a less bloody place if these rulers she was supposed to admire had read a novel or two once in a damn while!

On Wednesday, Alex Rice is not in class. Instead, he has sent her an e-mail message, informing her, in disheartening English, that he "had to catch a plane back to California for an overnite visit, do to unforescene circumstances." He was sorry, and "really hopped" she understood. "It will not hapen again."

The class and she too, she realizes, are subdued by this temporary loss, but Luis is not absent. The bodyguard, dressed this time in black jeans and a blue T-shirt with the college's name on the front, is waiting for her in the hall when she emerges after the last student has shuffled out of the room. He gives her a timid smile when she glances his way.

"Do you remember me?" he says. "I work for Alex Rice?"

"Yes, of course I remember you."

"Alex was sorry he couldn't come today but he had a family emergency back in California."

She looks at Luis, wondering what family he is talking about. Supposedly Alex Rice is childless. Or else he has missed the second class of the term because of his movie career, which, she imagines, plenty of people would have urged him not to walk away from. Next to the people who have made millions off of Alex Rice Inc. and ensured that he has done the same, what is she besides a grade dispensary—just one more woman to win over, one in a very minor role at that?

"He was hoping you could tell me what you guys went over in class today and then I could call and let him know so he won't get behind. "

"Is he really that worried about this class?" she asks, irritated.

His face flushes. "Um, I guess he is."

"It'd be best if he sent me an e-mail or came to see me during my office hours once he's back."

He opens his mouth then closes it. She can see that she has cowed him; somehow she has intimidated a two-hundred-pound bodyguard, one who looks like he could crack walnuts in his meaty fists. Despite how ineffectual she feels much of the time she stands in front of her students, it seems that she still has the ability to frighten or humble some people, the ones who might never have felt very comfortable in school or else were taught by their parents that teachers—like police officers and firefighters—always deserved their respect.

Luis shifts his weight from one foot to the other, both hands jammed in his pockets. Aside from the goatee, his face is boyishly smooth and unlined; she doubts that he is much older than her students. "Are you sure there isn't something I could tell him to do for Monday?"

"Everything he needs to know for our next class is on the syllabus. We're continuing the discussion of *Rabbit, Run* that we started today." She would like to be nicer to him but her resentment for Alex Rice, whom she guesses would never understand why he is imposing on her, is too strong.

"So there's no paper due?"

"No, not for another three weeks."

"Thank you, Professor. I'll be sure to tell him to come see you. Are you in your office on Friday?"

"I'm sometimes there in the morning," she sighs. "My office hours are listed on the syllabus. Why aren't you with him in California? Why didn't he choose a college out there in the first place?" The questions hang in the air before she can stop them, but Luis doesn't blink.

"I guess it's because he grew up here. I'm not really sure why. He didn't take me back to L.A. because he wanted to give me a couple of days off. He's got another guy. We switch off."

"Oh. I see."

"I've thought about taking classes here too," he says hopefully. "But it's kind of hard with my schedule."

She looks at him, her sour mood dissipating. His is the type of job she would never want, not in a thousand years. "I suppose it is, but you should still try."

"I'm going to, as soon as I can."

"Good," she says. "I have to get going now."

"Of course, ma'am. Sorry to keep you." He offers his hand, his palm cool and soft.

The man she is seeing now, the first since grouchy Peter, is a guitarist who teaches at a small music school and plays some weekends in a bluegrass band. She has known Milo for close to a year but has only been seeing him for two months; he is a few years older, divorced, kind. He thinks that it must be something like getting all three wishes at once to have a movie star in her class.

"It wasn't ever my wish," she says. "Maybe to date one, but not to teach one."

"Do you think you could tell him about the band? If he came to a show, people would find out he's a fan and I bet we'd get a boost from it."

"You're kidding, right?" she coughs, almost swallowing an unchewed bite of her lunch.

They are eating in a sub shop a few blocks from the music school, the little dining area crowded with men in business suits and teenagers in Cubs jerseys from a nearby high school. It is Thursday, the day after Alex's absence and the one weekday that she schedules for research, but she hasn't been doing much of it, despite having had the summer off, a stretch free of students and most departmental obligations. Instead, she spent most of her vacation reading for pleasure, taking books from her shelves that she had owned since college—short stories and novels, most written by European women, which has not helped her research because she is supposed to be writing about the female characters in early- and mid-twentieth century novels written by American male authors. Her plan has been to find a type that doesn't fit the mold of the spinster or the good-hearted whore or the castrating lover, or else the holdover from the Victorian era—matrons who viciously disdained other women who sought a life outside of their homes. But she can't find many convincing examples of female characters who are allowed to want more than what early-modern society condoned: childrearing and wifehood, or else the lonely nun or schoolmarm's fate.

Milo is disappointed. "No, I wasn't kidding. I just thought you could tell the whole class about one of my shows. Maybe he'd come if he thought you were going to be there. You don't have to tell him directly."

"If you were doing a poetry reading or something, I'd think about it, but not a concert. I'm sure he wouldn't go to impress me either."

"Why do you say that?"

She can't tell if he is teasing her. "Kate Winslet and Jessica Biel and I do not draw our dates from the same pool of men. No offense to you, of course."

"Kate Winslet hasn't dated Alex Rice, has she? Isn't she married?"

"You know what I mean."

"But what if he asked you out? Would you say yes?"

"I'm dating you," she says, feeling her stomach leap at his words. "And no, I would not go out with Alex Rice, even if he weren't my student. I'm not an idiot."

"I don't see why dating a movie star would make you an idiot."

"Because it would never last. He has women crawling all over him twenty-four hours a day. He's got a bodyguard sitting outside our classroom, and I don't think it's because he's afraid of getting shot."

"Are you serious? A bodyguard? That's so crazy. He has that guy with him all the time?"

"As far as I know, yes."

"Jesus, I couldn't imagine."

He is impressed with Alex Rice to a degree she hasn't expected. She had thought he would be mildly interested or else a little scornful, possibly jealous, not so admiring. But it makes sense to her now. He is, after all, a man who makes part of his living by playing music on a stage, with the hope of earning the respect and affection of strangers. It is the fame, she assumes, not so much Alex's millions, that he craves. The beautiful, available women too. He already has money; his family owns a chain of successful pancake houses in the suburbs. He also has talent. She knew upon first hearing him play that it was real, not just the product of her desire for him, which is sometimes very strong, sometimes barely there. She does not think that she is in love with him yet and isn't sure if he loves her, but he has become important to her. He is sincere about so much, whereas many people she knows are cynical, crabby, always ready for an argument. He is also willing to read whatever she gives him; he has told her that every book, in one way or another, helps with his songwriting. He swears that his curiosity is as valuable to him as his guitar-playing.

Despite the fact the semester is only a few days old, she feels exhausted. She has thought of Alex Rice's presence in her classroom with wearying frequency, her concentration often easily disrupted as it is. Her true nature has asserted itself, a condition that she has mostly kept at bay with scholarly busyness and books and friendships and everyday minutiae. Now, however, she knows herself to be a woman afraid of engagement, of exposure, of experience, of change, of strangers, of obsolescence and loneliness. She does not know how much she has lived, or what in fact living really means, other than the attempt to do things that inspire admiration and envy in others.

The next day is Friday and she is in her office early, pretending to do research for her book, which would be her second, the first having appeared four years ago, when she was twenty-nine and only a year into her tenure-track job. She was the department's trophy hire that year, and for a while was very doted on by the chair and one or two of the older faculty who were not prone to feeling threatened by her promise, which so far she knows she hasn't lived up to.

By noon, Alex Rice still has not appeared, and at one-thirty, when she is on the verge of slinking home in a self-lacerating snit, someone knocks on her door. Her witless heart seizes. Despite having checked it an hour ago, she wonders how much her lipstick has faded, if her perfume is too strong, but after she says, Come in, it is only the bodyguard who steps from behind the door. Her trembling smile freezes and she is certain that he knows he has disappointed her, something he must be used to in his career as a famous man's shadow.

He is dressed in a pale blue oxford shirt and khaki pants, and carries two shopping bags, one from Neiman Marcus, the other from Whole Foods. He is a good-looking man, taller than Alex by an inch or two, but of course his is not the face people recognize.

"I hope I'm not bothering you," he mumbles, unable to hold her gaze. "Alex is sorry he couldn't come today, but he wasn't able to get a flight back from L.A. until tonight." He stands uncertainly in the doorway.

Managing to smile, she motions for him to sit in the chair next to her desk. He settles the shopping bags at his feet and draws a beribboned white box out of the Neiman Marcus bag. "This is for you," he says, setting it on the desk.

She stares at the box. "That's very kind," she finally says, "but I can't accept gifts from students while they're enrolled in my class."

He looks confused, then embarrassed. She feels a stab of pity for him but knows she can't change her mind, despite her curiosity: how extravagant would a gift from Alex Rice be?

"It's not from Alex," he says. "It's from me. Can you take a gift from me? I promise it's not from Alex."

Her mouth goes dry. ". . . I'm not sure what the occasion is?"

"I just like giving gifts," he says, "now that I finally make money. That's all. I saw this when I was out earlier today and thought you would like it. I don't know many other people to give gifts to around here. Not yet."

Oh God, she thinks. He can't possibly have a crush on me, can he? "I'm very flattered that you wanted to give me a gift, but I really don't think that I can accept it."

His face falls. "Could you open it? Then see if you don't want it?"

Her heart is hammering hard when she takes the box and unties the ribbon. Inside is a lilac cashmere shawl, an enormous, marvelous piece of cloth that must have cost him a fortune. It is the most exquisite gift any man has ever given to her. She feels almost queasy and touches it reverently. She wants it very much but does not know how she could possibly keep it.

"It's magnificent, but I . . . it's not my birthday or anything," she says idiotically.

"Please, Professor Royce. I don't want to have to return it. If you like it, I think you should have—"

"Couldn't you send it to your mother? Or your sister?"

He laughs. "They live in L.A. They don't need scarves like this out there."

"Surely you have a girlfriend?"

He shakes his head. "Not right now. It's for you anyway." He gets up, picks up his grocery bag and is at the door before she has a chance to think of a reply.

"Please keep it," he pleads. "At least for a couple of days. If you still don't want it on Monday, you can give it back to me then. I don't mean to embarrass you or make you think I expect anything back from you. I just like giving gifts. If Alex were here, he'd vouch for me."

"I believe you, Luis. I do."

"I hope so," he says, and then he is gone.

She does not tell Milo about the shawl when she sees him that evening. She has brought it home, folded neatly in its gleaming white box, and stashed it in her closet, but it is like a live animal, the air and energy in her house altered by its presence. During dinner and the lovemaking that follows, she keeps wondering if her life has actually changed—has anything besides her consciousness been altered by the fact of the gift? It would seem not; it is the bodyguard, not the star, who has made this gesture.

After midnight, with Milo asleep beside her, she is still awake, wishing she hadn't taken the shawl because it will be very hard to return it to him. She realizes that she could take it back to Neiman Marcus instead—generous, apparently well-meaning Luis included a gift receipt in the box. But as soon as the thought surfaces, she quashes it. Never. She is not that kind of woman. She does not need the money and knows that she will have to give the shawl back, right away on Monday, after class, in front of Alex, unfortunately, but it has to be done. How could she keep it anyway—this declaration of intimacy from such an unusual (dangerous even, some might say) stranger?

Milo breathes next to her, shifting his head on the pillow, but he is sound asleep. She looks at him, touches his hair, which is wavy and brown and falls almost to his shoulders. He is a handsome man, one of the handsomest she has dated since college. She has imagined them becoming more serious if he stays in Chicago, if his band, The Windmills, doesn't move its home base. She doesn't really care about marriage or having children; she never has, something that makes her an amusing oddity to some of her friends, an enviable figure to others. And Milo has said that he doesn't want to marry again, at least not any time soon, his first marriage having been such a disaster, his wife having lied about stealing from him, which even at the end she wouldn't admit, despite the kited checks, the thousands she had taken from their household account to squander on the slot machines in an Indiana casino.

An hour later, she is no closer to sleeping. She goes on tiptoe to the closet and takes out the box, carrying it into the living room where she unties the ribbon and lifts the lid, the shawl swathed in white tissue paper. It is so beautiful that she would be afraid to wear it if she did keep it. She has no idea why Luis picked her, why he didn't choose some pretty young girl from one of Alex's other classes. Maybe, despite Luis's disclaimer, Alex *is* behind the gift, hoping to milk an unearned A out of her, or else advance credit for the absences that are sure to follow the one on Wednesday. She touches the fabric to her cheek and gathers the shawl in her arms, taking it to the sofa where she lies down and finally, falls asleep.

When she wakes hours later, it is to the sound of Milo making coffee in her sunny, messy kitchen. The shawl is in a heap on the floor, and she feels cold and guilty, stuffing it into its box. She brushes the hair out of her eyes and goes into the kitchen where her boyfriend looks up from the sink and smiles. "Was I snoring last night?" he teases.

She rubs the gooseflesh on her arms. "No, I couldn't sleep. I thought I'd get up and read for a little while but then I dozed off on the couch. I haven't done that in years. Sorry about that."

"You don't have to apologize. I hope you don't mind if I skip breakfast.

I'm meeting the guys in an hour to go over a few songs for tonight and have to stop by my place first. If I'd been thinking ahead, I would have brought my guitar with me."

"That's okay. I'm not hungry right now anyway."

"Are you still planning to come to the show tonight? I'd love it if you would."

"I'm planning on it."

"Good. I'd miss you if you didn't come."

He plays most weekends and she almost always goes, the bluegrass music much more fun than she had thought it would be. He has educated her too, taught her about the music's layers and complexities—it has more to offer than the hyped-up angst of most popular country-western music. And like zydeco, he has said, blue grass is tied inextricably to place, to its makers' individuality.

He kisses her and hands her a cup of coffee that is stronger than she likes but she drinks it, feeling the bitter black heat warming her body. No mention of the shawl and she is relieved, not sure if she would have told him the truth if he had confronted her. Most likely, if he noticed it at all, he thought nothing of it. He rarely comments on her clothes, which is sometimes exasperating.

After he is gone, she showers and sits at her desk and works on her book until her back is stiff and she is hungry and soon it is time to get ready to see Milo again. If she concentrates, she doesn't have to think about Alex or Luis or the gift. It is not so hard, and she is happy enough if she pauses to consider it. Perhaps Luis gave her a gift because he really did only want to spend money and she should stop being so suspicious and petty about it. She has a man in her life whom she cares about; she has a good job; she has ideas in her head that could lead to good work, to respect from her peers, and more good work. There is nothing for her to complain about, nothing at all.

Monday arrives very quickly, as it often does, and Alex Rice has returned. He is waiting for her in the hall outside their classroom, his movie-star skin glowing with good health and prosperity. He is so aggressively good-looking that it embarrasses her, makes her feel like she has big feet and bad teeth and limp hair. Luis is there too, an abashed smile on his face; he can barely look at her. Both he and Alex hold copies of *Rabbit, Run*. Oh no, she thinks, guessing what's coming.

Alex is the first to speak. Could Luis sit in on the class . . . he's done the reading, he'll be quiet, he'll sit in the back? Would it be all right, Professor Royce? Maybe not every class but maybe every other class? Alex's smile is fierce while Luis stares at the floor.

"No, no, I shouldn't have asked," Luis says, knowing what her hesitation means, not as bold as Alex in talking over resistance or ignoring it outright. "I still have to be enrolled to audit, don't I? I think you said the class was full and you don't let anyone extra sign up?"

"No, I don't," she says, trying to keep her voice even. She has the shawl with her, but not in the Neiman Marcus bag, not wanting to bring attention to it, to embarrass Luis by making an expensive show of it. A few students pass them on their way into the room, glancing at her and the two men, curious.

She could say yes. It really does not have to become a capital issue. She could let him sit in on her class, let him join the discussions, but the principle of it bothers her, especially in view of last Friday's events. She feels coerced, manipulated, even if Luis's embarrassment is as genuine as it seems to be.

"I'll just wait outside," he says. "I'm sorry to put you on the spot, Professor Royce. I shouldn't have asked."

"I asked," says Alex. "Not you."

She exhales audibly. "You can join us for today, but we'll have to see about including you in future classes. This isn't something the university condones."

"I don't want to get you in trouble," says Luis.

"No, no, don't worry about that." She glances at her watch. "We need to get started. Just come in and find a seat."

Alex chooses a desk in the front row, a few feet from her podium. Luis sits in a back corner, a few desks between him and the closest student. She is already sweating and wishes Alex were sitting in the back too, far enough away so that she might ignore his eyes on her. He has had his way, as he must be so used to doing. She looks back at Luis and smiles at him, intent on ignoring his famous employer, and for most of the class she does. But Alex Rice seems to have his eyes focused on her almost the whole time, willing her to look at him. When she does meet his gaze, it disorients her for a second. *It's him,* she thinks. *This man is actually Alex Rice.*

Before the class ends, she finds herself trying to turn back another insidious thought, but it persists. She wonders if he ever thinks of her in some context other than her classroom. She hates that she is so susceptible to him, to a man whose movies, the few she has seen, she uniformly disliked. Yet, in spite of his mediocre work, he is still a celestial body—beautiful and famous and rich. She is none of these things and cannot ever reasonably expect to be. It would be very easy to detest him if she could see past his celebrity and its sprawling implications.

He raises his hand often and at one point proclaims that Rabbit Angstrom is a jerk, little more than an overgrown boy who also seems to be a sex maniac. Doesn't he know how to control himself? He kind of seems to hate women too. What's that about? A few of the female students giggle. She can't suppress a smile and wonders if Luis suspects the irony of these words too, his eyes raptly on her whenever she turns his way, but he is too shy to speak in front of the other students who sit in their seats with the full weight of their official enrollment behind them. They belong, and of course some of them must know that he is an interloper.

By the end of class, she feels distinctly unsettled. She has the urge to comfort Luis, to tell him to take back the shawl and save his money. She wants to exhort him to do something else with his life, no matter Alex Rice's dazzling wealth, or the leftover women, or the thrill of jetting from one state, one continent, to the next with the expense of such rapid movement no hindrance. She wants to protect him, to save him, but from what, she isn't sure—his own obscurity? From the fact that Alex could easily replace him, hire some coarser man who has no interest in educating himself into a more worldly perspective or a different social class?

As everyone files out of the room, she loses her nerve. She keeps the shawl, says nothing to Luis as he shuffles behind Alex into the hall, not even that he is welcome to sit in on Wednesday's class too. She goes to her office where she sits in a cowardly funk for two hours before heading home. Once there she doesn't return the message Milo has left on the machine. When he shows up on her doorstep a little after ten, she lets him in and stumbles into his arms and starts crying. He looks at her in bewilderment and asks if she wants to break up with him.

"Of course not," she sobs. "It's not you at all."

He pulls back and looks at her. "It's that movie star, isn't it."

She shakes her head.

"You can tell me if it is."

"It's not him." Which is true enough, but she won't admit that he isn't far off. It is all so ridiculous—she now in a peculiar state of mourning for someone who a few days ago meant nothing to her. For someone who most likely would feel angry or insulted if he knew that he has inspired pity in her—because what kind of life does she have? What does she have that is so much better than the life he has started to make for himself?

"You don't have to tell me why you're upset, but if you want to, I'm willing to listen. I won't fly off the handle."

"It's okay," she says. "I know it'll pass. Please don't worry. I don't want us to break up."

"I've never seen you cry before."

"I don't do it that often."

"I'm glad we're together, Liz."

"You don't have to say that," she says, embarrassed.

"I know I don't."

"I'm glad we're together too."

He looks at her, uncertain.

"I should have told you before now," she says. "I do mean it, Milo."

On Wednesday, the fourth class of the term, Luis is absent. She worries she is responsible and wonders if she is being punished for not including him more willingly on Monday. Alex's face gives nothing away. He sits in the front row again, keeping a close eye on her, smiling often and with such delight that she wonders if he has taken something. He speaks frequently and is respectful of her and his classmates' opinions. He isn't a dimwit either, probably a B student, but she will know a lot more after she reads his first paper.

Another bodyguard is waiting in the hall, a thickly-muscled, stocky man named Morris, who with his boxy form and prematurely graying hair, reminds her of an elephant. Alex introduces her to him after class, just as he did on the first day with Luis.

"Where's Luis?" she asks.

The two men exchange a look before Alex answers. "Wednesday's his day off."

She hesitates. "But he was here last Wednesday."

He is still smiling, still as unruffled as he was in class. "That's because I asked him to meet with you after I got called to California. Which I'm sorry about. It was kind of hairy there for a day or two but everything's fine now."

She can see that he would explain himself if asked. "I wouldn't mind if he wanted to attend our classes."

"I'll let him know. That's very nice of you."

"He really would be welcome. Please be sure to tell him."

Alex and the elephantine Morris contemplate her for a long, unpleasant second. "He worried he was being too pushy," Alex finally says. "I don't know if he still wants to do it. I don't think he does."

She stares at him, ambushed by a feeling of needless loss. She has no idea what to say and nods at both men before turning away. They let her walk down the hall and out the doors, into the golden heat of early September, where at least a dozen students stand smoking cigarettes, hips cocked, feet splayed. Hardly any of them look at her. She is a teacher, a necessary nuisance in their trajectory through four years of sex and drinking and perfunctory study. She has read so many books in her life, knows these students so tragically well that her grief almost chokes her. What Alex Rice wants here will probably remain a mystery to her, but Luis, he is not that much of a mystery. He is the same as most of these students, as far as she can tell, an eye on the distant chance, one that recedes and approaches at unpredictable intervals. He is not so different from her. She could almost love him for this one pitiable fact.

Interview
with the
Second Wife

Eleven years ago, a young man traveled through four states to meet with me. It was a few months after Patric had died, and until yesterday, I don't think I had thought about this man in a few years. His name was in yesterday's paper, not on the front page, but this is a newspaper at least two or three million people read each day, and there was his picture, section 2, page 4, the story an unfortunate one. It seems he had plagiarized a large portion of one of his former students' dissertations and sent it off into the world as his own. The student had died two years ago, in a diving accident somewhere in Italy, but his girlfriend recognized the prose that Dr. Krenek had claimed to have written.

When we met, I wouldn't have thought he would be capable of such a disingenuous act. But it could be that I'm likely to assume the best about people who appear keenly interested in who I am, not just in who Patric was. In the years since we met, Dr. Krenek has become a professor of comparative literature at a very old and admired university in New England, and such scandals, I know, inevitably ruin careers, if not also lives.

His was the second professorial plagiarism scandal that this school had experienced in a year, and the tone of the article was overtly cynical. I've thought about writing and offering to help him, but I suspect that he wouldn't be happy to hear from me because if nothing else, it would alert him to the fact that yet another person knows of his crime, a person who had once been very close to a man whose work Dr. Krenek studied and admired. I also think he believed that I thought well of him during our short involvement, which I did, despite the sometimes puzzling evidence that he did not have all of his facts about Patric and me in good order when he arrived to conduct the interview, one I agreed to so that he might write his own dissertation, one that helped him secure the position at the university where he now finds himself in disgrace.

Some of the questions he asked me were extraordinary—because of their unexpectedness and because of his apparent ignorance of the reasons why two people decide to form a couple. I answered almost all of them, sometimes trying not to make a funny face or laugh at him outright. Having little experience with interviews, I didn't know if I was being foolish to find him odd or naive. He included portions of our conversation in his dissertation, which met with some acclaim after he published it with a university press in Chicago. When I read the excerpts of our interview in his book, I wondered if he might never have had any intention of using those strange questions and instead only wanted to satisfy some prurient element of his curiosity about Patric (and myself? It's hard to know if in Dr. Krenek's view, I represented much more than an extension of Patric, something, like his books, that he had left behind).

After reading the newspaper article, I unearthed my copy of the interview transcript, which I had managed not to misplace in the move I made eight years ago from the house where Patric and I lived in western New Jersey to the apartment where I now live in New York. Aside from making me feel an oppressive melancholy for my old life, I regret that Dr. Krenek has gotten himself into trouble. Of course plagiarism is a shameful crime and certainly one of the most invasive, but I don't think it deserves the kind of outrage it often inspires. His case should be the concern solely of his publisher and his employer, not the fuel for more media sensationalism.

We only saw each other twice. He had a tape recorder with him both times he came to the house, but managed to get it working only on the

second day because that first day, he hadn't realized the batteries would give out a few minutes into our conversation. I realize he must seem a bumbler. Maybe it was the state of mind he found me in those two afternoons that allowed me to attribute attractive qualities to him—perhaps I was merely lonely and relieved to have someone in the house again (one with three floors and too much chilly space for a childless woman), someone close to my age and not related to Patric or his life in France before he'd known me. I cannot say why I felt as I did. But I immediately liked Dr. Krenek, who at the time went only by Sylvan, an unusual name that seemed very lovely to me.

Patric's last two books, *Land of Sappho* and *The Bus Kept Going,* were to be the focus of Dr. Krenek's dissertation, and they were the most controversial of the ten he had published, in part because they were so different from his earlier novels—in both their structure and their unapologetic eroticism. I wonder if I should have taken one of Patric's colleague's advice and had a friend sit with me during the interview to ensure that Dr. Krenek did not overstep any boundaries—whatever they were supposed to be. But I chose not to, and I don't regret it, though it might have been interesting, if such a thing had been possible, to see if he would have asked fewer questions about Patric's and my personal lives and more about Patric's work if we had had a chaperone.

Dr. Krenek's prefatory notes:
Interview with Cynthia Lewis, Washington Crossing, NJ, home of the late Patric Lorieux and Ms. Lewis, February 16 & 17, 1996. What follows is the official transcript of our conversations. Due to technical difficulties with the recording device, the majority of the interview occurred on February 17.

SK: How long were you and Mr. Lorieux together before he died?

CL: Just a little over thirteen years.

SK: You were once his student?

CL: Yes, we met when I was enrolled in his nineteenth-century French novels course at NYU.

SK: How old were you?

CL: Almost twenty-three.

SK: And Mr. Lorieux was fifty-five at the time?

CL: Yes, I think he was.

SK: So you're his second wife. I've always wondered what it would be like to be the second. I'd worry that the first act would be too hard to follow. (Laughs). Not that this was the case with you and Mr. Lorieux. When did you marry him?

CL: I'm not his second wife. We were never married. We only lived together.

I remember how surprised I was by this question. I had no idea why he thought we'd been married. It's possible he did know and instead wanted me to say why Patric had never married me or why I hadn't married him, however he would have phrased it. But he didn't ask. We were sitting on the worn leather sofa in the living room, the bay window behind us, one that overlooked an enormous maple tree. No snow on the ground, only a brown, muddy lawn below the tree's skeletal branches. Despite the strange question, I felt stupidly excited and nervous facing him, his dark eyes very serious, his voice sometimes cracking a little.

SK: But you are his literary executor?

CL: Yes.

And I have remained his executor, even though his ex-wife, the ambitiously named Victoire, eventually tried to take me to court to overturn Patric's dictum. This was something Patric predicted and I had met his attorney in case I needed her while the will was in probate. He had the will drawn up in the U.S. in order to make it harder for Victoire to assail it, and he had also been naturalized a few years before his death. It was his foreignness that had initially attracted me to him, along with his books, of course. He spoke very good English but his French accent never disappeared and each of the many times we went to France together, almost twenty trips, I found myself newly smitten with him. His friends loved him and never tired of seeing him, and they were kind to me, despite whatever loyalties they might have retained for Victoire. Patric was a celebrity there—we were treated to magnificent meals and late-night receptions in Parisian homes where decisions that affected the entire country were made. He was tall for a Frenchman too, close to six feet—from across many crowded rooms with inscrutable family portraits on their walls, I remember seeing his head with its wild tufts of gray hair rising

from the darker heads clustered around him. For a long time, he was the most romantic figure I had ever seen.

SK: One thing that struck me in Mr. Lorieux's final book was how he was able to create a realistic society governed exclusively by women. In the main character Isabelle, we see a woman who wears women's clothes but puts on a beard in the scenes where she addresses her constituents. I think Mr. Lorieux was actually satirizing masculinity rather than having his female characters bow to it, but others have interpreted Isabelle's behavior as a kind of submission to the model of a patriarchal society. If women wanted to govern, they had to look like men. Which of these two interpretations would you say is closest to what the author intended?

CL: More than anything else, the women in beards were meant to be darkly comic. They were meant to underscore the absurdity of giving one person, male or female, so much power over so many others. I can't believe there's any confusion about this. *Land of Sappho* was a satire. Even the title alludes to this, don't you think?

SK: But there's no reason why we should automatically assume it's a satire based on the title alone. Maybe if he had called it *Isle of Lesbos* instead. Not everyone knows that Sappho lived there. Was he hoping to style himself a feminist?

CL: He was a feminist. No question.

I remember wanting either to laugh or shout at him at that moment. I wondered if he had misread the entirety of Patric's work, not just *Sappho.* It was an unusual book in that it rivaled *Brave New World* for its political astuteness, but it was as funny as *Lucky Jim.* I see other parallels among them too—Huxley and Amis were Brits; Patric was French—no American could have written *Sappho,* according to Patric. It was too subtle, he said, not exactly with modesty. He thought Americans expected women to be three things—saints, sluts, or ciphers. In *Sappho,* the women were no less complicated than the men—both sexes were complex, contrary creatures who privately questioned every violent death, even if their rhetoric made it seem like violence was an absolute necessity, if not an absolute good.

SK: I've never thought he was a true feminist. He seemed to respect women but he didn't really trust them, did he?

CL: It was people he didn't trust. Not just women.

SK: Did he want to have children with you?

CL: I'm not sure how this pertains to Patric's work.

SK: I guess what I'm wondering is whether he wanted to put you in a submissive role. When a woman agrees to carry a man's child, she's automatically making herself vulnerable to the man.

CL: You could also say that the man is making himself vulnerable to the woman. Just in a different way.

SK: But you can't deny that pregnancy is harder on women. They exist within the pregnant state in a more immediate way than men do. They can't walk away and forget for a day or a week that they're carrying a child.

CL: A man might be able to separate himself physically from the pregnancy, but he can't deny the fact that he had a major role in impregnating the woman and now has a major responsibility toward her and their unborn child. Our laws, if nothing else, make this the case.

SK: (clearing his throat): Mr. Lorieux wrote so well about children in his novels, especially in *The Shaded Pond*. He seemed to have had an uncanny understanding of how they see the world.

CL: He was a child once himself, of course. (Laughs). And no, we never talked seriously about having children together.

This was a lie. We had tried to have a child, but my body had rejected the idea, more than once. This was hard on both of us, but I saw no reason to tell Sylvan any of this. I'm sure there are quite a few moments in any couple's life together that are best left unexposed to general scrutiny, no matter that Patric was a public figure, and in our age, public figures are not meant to have private lives. I know that he hadn't blamed me for the miscarriages but the fact that he could do nothing about them, even less than I might have been able to, made him angry. "Someone so young," he had said after the second one, "Someone so young as you should never have to worry about a thing like this. It's fucking unfair, Cynthia." He could never pronounce the th in my name, the French having no equivalent. My name always sounded like Sint-zia in his mouth.

SK: Did he believe in God?

CL: No, not always.

SK: Would you mind elaborating?

CL: He sometimes experienced intensely spiritual moments when he felt that something aside from exploding stars and black holes were out there in the universe, something sentient and possibly benevolent, but eventually he would think of his father who was murdered for his role in the French resistance, and he'd say that he couldn't believe in God or something godlike because he didn't believe in Santa Claus or the frog prince either. What he believed in more than anything else was absurdity. Chaos, I guess.

SK: I don't think chaos is the same thing as absurdity. Absurdity is sixty clowns emerging from one car, whereas chaos is sixty clowns in one car colliding with sixty clowns in another car. Forgive the sophomoric analogy, but I think it's apt.

CL: They both sound absurd to me. I don't know. Absurdity is what he probably believed in the most.

What came next was possibly the most disturbing moment in the whole interview, at least in its initial, visceral effect on me:

SK: If Patric had had to choose between the following, under penalty of death, would he have had his eyes gouged out or his penis cut off?

I remember staring at him for several seconds after he asked me this, wondering if he was kidding, but he didn't seem to be. It almost felt like he'd slapped me. Imagining Patric without his eyes or his penis? I would rather have imagined him dead. But maybe it's easy for me to say this because he already was dead.

CL: He would rather have had his hands cut off.

SK: That wasn't one of the choices.

CL: Then I'd prefer not to answer. I have no idea. I doubt he would have answered either if he'd been here to speak for himself.

SK: I know it sounds perverse, but it's actually a question Marie-France asks Jean de Vosges in *The Bus Kept Going*.

CL: Oh, I didn't remember that.

SK: I would think it'd be impossible to forget.

CL: If I had a penis maybe it would be.

SK: Jean said that he'd rather have his eyes gouged out.

CL: Oh. I don't know if that's what Patric would have chosen for himself, but maybe.

SK: I bet he would have. The penis is often a metonym for man. (Long pause). I hope you'll forgive me if my questions seem a little rude sometimes. You weren't what I was expecting. I've seen photos of you but I wasn't . . . I wasn't prepared for how pretty you are in person. I'm sorry to embarrass you by saying such a thing, but I want you to know that if I seem a little brusque, it's only a defense mechanism. That must sound a little ridiculous, but it's true.

Like a desperate fool, I blushed. I believed what he was saying, even though I understood that flattery might only have been one of his interviewer's tools (perhaps the only effective one he had), meant to disarm me and bring about more personal revelations. It might also have been a precursor to the impulse or compulsion that led him to steal his student's work. Such an impulse could already have been alive in him.

CL: You don't have to defend yourself against me.

SK: Logically I know that, but *le coeur a ses raisons que raison ne connait point.* You do speak French?

CL: Yes.

SK: The heart has reasons that reason doesn't know.

CL: Yes, I know.

SK: Before you, did Mr. Lorieux date other women so much younger than him?

CL: Yes, I think he did.

SK: How old was the youngest?

CL: I'm not sure. Maybe nineteen or twenty? I don't really remember. He didn't talk that much about his old lovers. I was the one he ended up leaving his wife and sons for. I don't think the other women were that important to him.

SK: Were you jealous of them?

CL: No, not all. It wasn't like that. We simply got along very well and then things changed and rather suddenly we were a couple. I hadn't taken his class with the intention of turning the famous visiting writer into my lover. He must also have been looking for something different, someone different.

sk: And that was you.

cl: Yes, I guess it was.

sk: Do you ever speak to Madame Lorieux?

cl: I saw her at the memorial service Patric's friends had for him in Paris. That was the last time I spoke with her. There was never very much for us to say to each other. We hadn't talked when Patric was alive, except when she called to discuss their sons' visits with him and I happened to answer the phone.

sk: Frenchwomen have a reputation for looking the other way if their husbands have mistresses. You probably know that François Mitterand had two families and both his wife and his mistress attended his funeral. Adultery isn't as much of a sin in France as it is here. The French don't believe that one person can be all things to his or her partner.

cl: I don't think she was at all indulgent when it came to him having a mistress. I think she knew when he had lovers, and I'm sure it bothered her. But as long as he kept coming home to her and their sons, I suppose she felt that she had to put up with it.

The abortive literary executor lawsuit hadn't yet come into play at the time of our interview. But even when Victoire was threatening me with it, we didn't see each other. Having the Atlantic Ocean between us certainly helped—in the end, she didn't have enough money to carry out a lawsuit that stretched from one continent to another. She might have won the case if she had had the resources, but I know she wouldn't have been as attentive to the executive demands of his estate as I have been. One could say that she missed the last thirteen years of his life, and as a result, probably spent much of this time despising him and me too, I suppose. It would not have surprised me if in turn she had made herself despise his books.

sk: What about when you two were together. Did he have a mistress?

cl: No.

sk: You're sure.

cl: Yes, I'm sure.

sk: How do you know?

cl: Because we talked about it. He promised to tell me if he ever desired someone else in that way.

sk: You don't think he would have lied?

cl: No, he wouldn't have. He didn't lie about that sort of thing.

Maybe I expected these questions. I must have. The fact that he wanted to know how I felt about Patric's interest in much younger women—this was nothing new. I had girlfriends who had warned me that I wouldn't last long because Patric had such an "unbelievable" ego that he would constantly need new admirers. This was what they thought, in any case. Some of their unkindness was obviously nothing more than corrosive female jealousy. I tried to ignore it, but a couple of my friendships eventually ended and Patric felt bad for me, but I suspected that he must also have been flattered to have us fighting over him. My parents were cynical about him too and sometimes harsh; I didn't see them very often while Patric and I were together—maybe once or twice a year, although they only lived a few hours' drive away. But my mother did like Patric, was charmed by him and his wit and intelligence, not to mention his good looks. He was a year older than her and she too must have been attracted to him. It was hard not to be. She has never admitted this, however.

sk: What is your relationship with his sons like now?

cl: We're friendly. They're both in their twenties and one is a writer but he hasn't published a book yet. He writes for *L'Express* sometimes and his articles are usually very good, but the two novels he's tried to publish haven't been picked up. I know he's frustrated by this but his father wrote three novels before he was able to publish one. I don't know if this comforts Julien very much, but he hasn't given up yet.

sk: What was Mr. Lorieux's relationship with his sons like? As you probably know, father and son relationships are a feature of several of his books, and the one in *The Bus Kept Going* is its centerpiece. For one year, Jean and his son Paul share Marie-France's bed on alternating nights. Was this ménage à trois based on real-life events?

cl: No, of course not. Not on my real life, that's for sure.

sk: You sound a little defensive.

cl: Well, I don't mean to. If what you're really asking is whether or not Patric ever asked me to share myself with Julien and Georges, he never did. He wrote fiction and always intended his readers to see it this way. His essays had some autobiographical elements, but his fiction was made up, as fiction obviously is supposed to be.

I began to wonder then if he was hoping to seduce me. Ineptly, but the mood of combative confession, his tone, his interested gaze—somehow the encounter seemed to have taken on the tenor of a seduction. Not long after we had started the interview, he had removed his sport jacket, a navy wool crested coat that made him look like the assistant maitre-d' for a WASPy country club, but he was not a WASP; he looked nothing like one with his large dark eyes and brows and knobby, hairy wrists and hands. He slouched against the sofa a little, as if ashamed of himself for being tall. Throughout our talk, he leaned toward me, holding the little corded microphone between us as we spoke, his face open and apparently guileless, even as he asked the more daring questions. After the sport coat was cast off, he loosened his tie and later removed it; he unbuttoned the top two buttons of his shirt, then rolled up his sleeves, his forearms shockingly hairy, but I liked this. I liked men with hair on their arms and chests, on their legs too, and I could imagine that Sylvan's legs were hairy, the long, thin length of them under his dark corduroy trousers furred by the biological imperatives of his masculine body. He was the first man since Patric had died whom I felt desire for. But I did not want to feel desire for him. At that moment in my life, it had seemed that it would be best not to desire any man ever again. I had work that I wanted to do—I wanted to write my own books, and lust would only have waylaid me further. I had been waylaid by thirteen years of domesticity with Patric and although I had been very happy for most of that time, I had also been younger than I was now. For thirteen years, I had been his lover, housekeeper, secretary, friend, and finally, his nursemaid. It had been an arrangement we had never discussed formally—it had simply happened, as so many things now seemed to have done, and I was very efficient at taking care of a number of tasks that he had needed assistance with.

SK: I don't mean to imply that he wrote anything but fiction, but you can't deny that many writers are inspired by the events of their own lives. It's not like I assume he was communicating with St. Teresa of Avila like Gerard in *House of Plenty*, or ever tried to make himself immune to hemlock like Isabelle, but you must understand that a reader naturally wonders how close the author is to his characters and their experiences.

CL: I understand all of that, but in this case, the threesomes were most decidedly fiction.

SK: How long did Patric need to be alone each day? Several of his peripheral characters definitely have hermetic tendencies, and they're often attributed with noble qualities too. I wonder if like Rousseau, he thought that man . . . and woman too, should aspire toward noble savageness—to be both learned and self-sufficient, and also live close to nature.

CL: He wasn't like Rousseau at all. He preferred to be in the house. He never camped a day in his life, as far as I know, and he wasn't interested in hunting or fishing. He liked people and he liked to socialize very much. We had dinner parties every fall and spring, and until the last year of his life, he held salons in our home. His students and colleagues and other writers he knew in the area were constantly in and out of our house during the school year. He liked to say that he wanted to be the local Gertrude Stein, but with gin martinis instead of pot brownies.

He didn't cut himself off from the world when he was writing either. His novels came out very fast. The last three did, anyway. He wrote during the summers, often at night while I slept because he went through long periods of insomnia. He'd spend the days napping and reading when he wasn't teaching. I'm sorry if my answers disappoint you, but I don't want to lie to make it seem more romantic than it really was.

SK: I don't think it's unromantic. Not at all. But you must have had other men interested in you who could have offered you things that Patric couldn't due to his more advanced age. Why did you stay with him for thirteen years?

CL (laughs): What do you mean why did I stay with him? What do you think? I stayed because I loved him.

SK: I don't doubt that you loved him, but in all that time, wasn't your head ever turned by someone else? Wouldn't he have been aware that you had other admirers and said something about it to you? Maybe as he got sicker he even suggested that you take a lover?

CL: My head wasn't turned by someone else. It really wasn't. I might have noticed good-looking men from time to time but I didn't want to pursue them or be pursued by them. Patric did say something once in a while if he noticed that someone had a crush on me, but there was no question that he would have condoned me taking a lover. He just wouldn't have. He was very possessive, even though he wasn't open about this tendency. He preferred to pretend that I could keep my own schedule, provided I was there at the times when he needed me, which toward the end was all the time. I won't pretend that I always liked this. We hired a nurse who eventually came to stay with us, but for a few months, I did most of the caregiving and it wore on us both very badly. He insisted on his privacy though and didn't want a stranger to witness the humiliation of his demise. But finally, it became too hard for me to manage on my own and he would rather have killed himself than go into a nursing home.

He changed during those last several months. But I don't think there's anyone who wouldn't have. I changed too, in that I realized that I was not so young anymore and would not have the same opportunities I'd once believed were my due. I didn't think there would be any children, and there haven't been, though I must not have wanted them that badly, even with Patric, which is fortunate, considering that he was only sixty-eight when he died. He lost his good nature, most of his muscle mass and all of his hair in those last months, and he was so ashamed of his body's brutal decline that he became bitterly angry. Not all of the time, but on some days I couldn't talk to him because he only shouted until he started coughing or retching and then he'd get this terrible stricken look and wouldn't say a word. In the last month, he didn't speak for five days in a row, and I really thought that I would go crazy. But then the week before he died, he changed again, returned to being the man he'd always been, and every hour that he was lucid he'd tell me he loved me, that I'd been the grace note of his life, that he was sorry he was dying, and this remains the saddest thing that I have lived through.

SK: Before you met him, what had you intended to be?
CL: A writer. I still intend to be a writer.
SK: Have you started to write now that you're free?
CL: I was free to write then too. But I didn't.

SK: That might have been very hard to do. Two writers often make for an antagonistic pair. Look at Hemingway and Martha Gellhorn. Some would say she was the better writer.

CL: No one would have said I was better than Patric.

SK: He did have more experience, but if you had been publishing at the same time, you can't know for sure what people would have said.

CL: There wasn't much risk that I ever would have eclipsed him.

SK: But now there is.

CL: Hardly.

He reached out here with the hand that wasn't holding the microphone and touched my arm. I looked down and kept staring at his hand until he withdrew it. He didn't apologize. I realized at that point that he could have done anything he wanted to me; I wouldn't have been able to fend him off, but I knew he wasn't going to press himself on me unless I made it clear that I was willing. It would have been very easy to go to bed with him, and I have to admit I thought about it. He was sexy and masculine and it had been more than a year since I had been touched in any kind of sensual way. But I was out of the habit and frankly, the prospect frightened me. Where would we have done it? Certainly not in the bed I had once shared with Patric, and I couldn't have done it on the floor or the sofa. It would have seemed too squalid. We had a guest room but the sheets hadn't been changed since the nurse had left and surely would have smelled musty. I didn't want my first time with a new man to be spoiled by these problems. I kept looking at my burning arm until he broke the silence by asking another question.

SK: What is your favorite memory of Mr. Lorieux?

CL: (long pause): I know this isn't what you mean, but he wrote me a number of poems and letters and they're all very dear to me. Aside from what they are on the page, they bring to mind the occasions when I received them. But there are other things, of course, and maybe this isn't my favorite memory, but it's one I used to think of pretty often. It happened on a day when I'd been teaching a class on Shakespeare at the local arts center. We'd been reading *Antony and Cleopatra,* and when I got home, Patric came out of his study wearing a breastplate and a toga, a bouquet of daisies in one hand and a fake sword in the other. (Laughs.) He stood staring at me for a long time, very serious, while I giggled and turned red, and then he recited two of my favorite lines from the play, "There's not a minute of our lives should stretch / without some pleasure now." It was so sweet and funny that I started crying. I had no idea where he'd gotten the costume. It was long past Halloween, so I knew he couldn't have gone to a costume shop. He wouldn't tell me where he'd gotten it until a few weeks later. I had to guess and guess, and it turned out that a friend who'd been a costumer in New York had lent it to him just so he could do this little thing for me.

SK: When he was in good health, it must have been wonderful to be with him. You must miss him terribly.

CL: Yes, sometimes I do. A lot of the time.

SK: I'm sorry if I've upset you. This must be hard. I know he hasn't been gone very long.

CL: You haven't upset me. I agreed to meet with you, so you don't have to apologize.

SK: I still feel like I should.

CL: Really, there's no need.

The interview went on for a little longer, but he stuck mostly to Patric's books and teaching after this. When we finally stopped, it was late, almost the dinner hour, and I invited him to stay for a meal and he accepted. I think we had a green salad and some spaghetti, nothing elaborate. I know we had some wine too, and when I stood up to take our plates into the kitchen, he stood up with me and put his hands on my shoulders and lowered his face to kiss me. I put the plates down and was shaking almost violently and he pulled me against his chest and I could smell red wine and warm male skin and I would have gone to bed with him then if he had tried to undress me. But he didn't. He held me against his chest until I stopped shaking and then he said he had better go because he didn't really know what he was doing. It was too soon, he said. He said that in the morning I would think that he had taken advantage of me because he had made me answer so many personal questions and Patric was someone he respected so much that he didn't think he should make love to his grieving widow. I told him that I wasn't Patric's widow but he said that basically I was and he needed to leave before he embarrassed himself further. He gathered up his things and left very abruptly and I mechanically put the plates in the sink and ran water over them and then I went into the living room where he had sat with me for half of the day and I couldn't sleep that night.

Now he has embarrassed himself for real—the public's judgment is decisive, and whether or not the university fires him, which I suppose is almost inevitable, he has no hope of putting this incident behind him. At least not any time soon, because he has abused their trust in a way that is as humiliating for them as it is for him. I feel very sorry for him—I do not know why he did it, but it is possible that his student's work would not have been written if Sylvan had not helped him find his way to this idea and shepherded him all the way through to its final pages. The student's work, Sylvan might have believed, should not have died with him. The girlfriend or whoever might have helped publish it posthumously, perhaps had no intention of doing so.

There are many possible reasons, *le coeur a ses raisons*. But few, very few, are ever decipherable.

Did I go on to write, as it seemed I was meant to? I cannot say that I have. I might have tried but I did not keep trying. Two years after Patric died, I went back to school for a fine arts degree. I had always known how to draw but hadn't cultivated this skill very much. I now do illustrations for medical textbooks; it is a very exacting discipline, and I like how beautifully precise every figure must be.

There was another man not long after Sylvan and I met. He was only a few years older than I and we were together for several years. Then another man arrived, but now again, I live alone. It would be easy enough to find Sylvan and tell him that I would like to help him get past all of this. But there seems little point. He doesn't write about Patric anymore. He is interested in Brecht—drama now instead of novels. He is balding and is recognizably older, judging from the photo in the newspaper, which of course does not show him to his best advantage. It is a strange thing to see someone you once wanted but in the end, didn't pursue. We never spoke again after that night. He wrote to me three times, once to thank me, once to send the transcript, and then finally, to send a copy of his book, *The Erotic-Political Dialectic in the Late Novels of Patric Lorieux*. Each of those three times I could have written back to him, but I did not know what he would have wanted me to say.

For Once
in Your Life

Sunday was the day of arguments. Most of the time people stood up to argue too—there was no prim bickering across the table or the room. They had held in grudges and suspicions all week, and after church, with those who went or not, the complaints came out in a bitter torrent. Sunday was not a day of rest with casseroles and long naps, nor of peace and contemplative behavior. It was a day of snits, as far as Lynne could tell, some of them nearing viciousness, a day of blaming and berating, of accusing others of acting loose with hard-earned money, not to mention other people's spouses and lovers. Her town had its share of mistresses and misters, but most people talked about this fact askance, saying it from the sides of mouths, eyes sly, sneers twisting lips into thin little scars. They would sooner wear a car tire around their necks than say that they could maybe see the point, that such things happened everywhere, and no one was strictly terrible for doing what they did without their clothes and front-porch manners. In her opinion, there were more than two sides in most debates, and most questions couldn't be answered with a simple yes or no. She had talked about this with Connie Fox, who was her hairstylist and not the person to get too philosophical with, as it turned out. As punishment for Lynne's willingness to argue for a third point of view, Connie Fox cut her bangs too short and later told the other women in the beauty parlor that she was an atheist, which wasn't true and Lynne had later said so, but she didn't know if anyone had believed her.

She had moved to Gull Harbor because it was next to an enormous lake and she liked water birds and sailboats and was also at the end of a long, tense separation from a job and a marriage she had grown tired of, a separation that she had wanted but her husband had not. She had always lived in polluted cities and had promised herself in the last one that the next time she moved, it would finally be to Gull Harbor where she had vacationed for four summers in her teens. She had gotten married right after college, had followed her husband to Orlando, to Los Angeles and finally to Chicago where she had left him and then had taken a year to get everything in order before moving to the town where she had learned to sail and swim.

Her job in Gull Harbor was officially a bookseller, unofficially a bookkeeper. On top of managing the local historical society's bookstore and café, she did the payroll for two physicians and a dentist, which was similar to the job she had done in her former life as a married woman and city dweller. Because she worked with a few of the professionals in town, she was considered a semi-professional. People seemed to like her, in part because she had been touched by the minor celebrity of the town's prescription-writers and bestowers of Novocain and fluoride rinses. She was invited to brunches, anniversary parties and baptisms. This was the main reason why she knew the big fights were saved for Sundays. Mondays too were rarely boring. The historical society hosted a biweekly Monday luncheon for the Gull Harbor's Women's Association, which she hadn't joined, but the luncheons were in the café and took over the whole space for two hours every other week. Several dozen Gull Harbor women were members; at least two dozen could be counted on to attend most luncheons.

The women, elaborately dressed and made up, marveled, whispered, snickered, drank, hooted, chuckled, teased, groused, and sometimes they sang, which Lynne disliked because they sounded pained and high-pitched, and sometimes they chose hymns and although she wasn't an atheist, these songs were best heard in a church, not the antique interior of a café serving half-carafes of wine, mushroom quiches and chicken Kievs.

Nonetheless, the women's gossip amused her with its often silly prejudices and quasi-scandals. She had heard much worse in her former big cities. She had seen much worse, and had been part of a very small scandal herself, the one with her husband Kris and the divorce no one in their families had understood the need for. There had been no other man, no abuse, nothing truly wrong except that to her mind, it had ended—like a pretty good movie, one she hadn't regretted seeing, as she had told Kris, who hadn't liked the analogy. Things had fallen flat and then she had fallen out of the habit. It perhaps had been cruel of her because he had treated her well, and remembered the things he should have remembered; he had been a strict observer of the social contract. He wasn't really boring either, but had become uninteresting. It had saddened her but she had felt there was no other option than to leave him. Near the end, she had said he could slap her face if it would make him feel better, but he had looked at her in outrage and told her that she was crazy. She hadn't thought he would do it either, but had wanted to see if it were possible.

The scandal under discussion at the mid-May luncheon, amid this month of tulips, college graduations and a few newborns, was one that had been the source of a particularly dramatic Sunday argument in the Wright household on Fourth Street. Mrs. Wright, a Women's Association member who had let her dues lapse, was having sex on Thursday afternoons with her chiropractor's middle son, both of them married, the age difference so great as to inspire more wonder than contempt. Brenda Wright was sixty, the son thirty-seven. He could be *her* son! Yes, she taught yoga at one of Gull Harbor's two gyms and was rather svelte; nevertheless, she was still too old.

It was the Thursday afternoons that got to Lynne. Only on Thursdays? How did they know this? She also wondered whom Brenda Wright had entrusted with this information. Maybe someone had stood outside of the Wrights' windows and eavesdropped? It had been done before, though this information-gathering technique had created its own scandal in the recent past, as had the keystroke-tracking software three husbands had installed on their wives' computers. This had seemed a terrible trespass—even the most moralistic WA members had been rattled by such secret police tactics.

Besides being a hairdresser, Connie Fox was a Women's Association member and served as its treasurer. She almost always attended the luncheons and was a key source of gossip because her beauty salon acted as the sieve through which many of the town's rumors were sifted. Because Lynne tipped her too much and had helped her with her income taxes, Connie had forgiven her their disagreements. Lynne hadn't really forgiven her but kept this to herself. Despite the fact Connie had known suffering—a year earlier she had lost a son in a war she hadn't supported—this suffering had not softened her. Suffering hadn't appeared to embitter her either, however. She took more sick days and did not tolerate talk about the war in her salon, but Lynne hadn't noticed any other changes. Connie still liked activity and social uproar; she dressed in the same bright blouses and dark slacks and seemed to ignore her husband's more noticeably altered state. Some nights he did not come home from work; he had a hunting cabin an hour north of Gull Harbor where it was said that as a hobby he built small wooden knickknacks for craft fairs. On the town streets, he was often seen with whiskers, his shirt untucked, receipts and to-do lists falling from his pockets. He was milder than his wife and always had been, but he was vaguer now too, as if thinking and rethinking a riddle he would probably never solve.

Regarding Brenda Wright, Connie said, "She wants a longer leash, not a divorce. Can you believe her nerve?"

"What does Rick want?" asked Marietta Sprink, a doctor's wife who still sometimes worked as an X-ray technician.

"A divorce," said Connie, "which he'll get on his terms."

"That means she won't get much money, if any," said Marietta.

"Probably not. But who can blame him?"

No one could, and as Lynne listened to the eruptions and sniggers as she helped the waitresses take away dirty plates and refill water glasses, she wondered if the son was the one who had leaked the news. Was he in love? It was said that he had been taking her yoga classes for a year, his wife with him at times, and all the while he had been nursing a serious crush on the soft-voiced, leotard-wearing woman of the warrior and bow poses.

"Are you sure this really happened?" someone asked, a woman whose name Lynne couldn't remember—Betsy? Brynne? a large-eyed, narrow woman who was a new WAM, one who hadn't yet petrified into her sanctioned WAM role.

The other women paused to regard her, almost mildly. Marietta laughed. "Of course we're sure."

Lynne could read the newcomer's face, which said, "Should I avoid her?" But the new WAM remained silent, despite the urgent question.

In Gull Harbor, however, real and terminal ostracism didn't seem to happen except in truly remarkable cases—ones involving bloodshed, rape, beaten children or wives, embezzlement of municipal funds. Lynne had rarely seen the WAMs moved to hatred—envy, yes; outrage, certainly. But some almost idolized the Brenda Wrights and definitely were infatuated with their daring.

A second-tier scandal was also under discussion, one concerning a pair of fourteen-year-old boys who had been caught committing a lewd act in a department store. They had each put on a dress from the store's racks, hidden in separate chambers in the ladies' dressing room and flashed the first women who stumbled upon them. It was a prank, they later claimed, a dare that their friends had put them up to. Connie's fifteen-year-old daughter and one of her friends had been two of the victims. Instead of finding it hilarious, as some of the less buttoned-up WAMs did, Connie thought it deviant behavior. "Those two boys will grow up to be dangerous perverts, if they aren't already."

"If they aren't yet perverts, they're certainly cross-dressers," Lynne couldn't help saying as she put a slice of lemon tart in front of Petra Lipman, the Women's Association vice-president. Several of the women laughed, their open mouths showing the handiwork of Dr. Epps, the town's handsomest dentist. He was also divorced.

Connie looked over at her. "Shelley was too young to see a boy's privates. That's one more thing she has to live with that no one can undo."

"The poor thing," said Marietta, her lips twitching.

Connie nodded. "The list is getting so long."

Lynne's bangs were still too short and she wanted to blurt, "You just wish it'd been you in there instead," but she went back to the kitchen and looked with violence at the coffee cups she would soon help carry into the dining room. One of the cups was chipped and she arranged to have the younger waitress give it to Connie. The girl nodded, saying nothing. Lynne doubted she would ever be above acts of pointless revenge. They were what some people lived for; in her case, they were one of the rarely exercised perks of her petty power at the historical society. Ever since the atheist rumor, she had thought about going to another hair salon but hadn't found the nerve. The town's population was a little more than seven thousand people—hardly tiny but small enough that such changes were noted and considered statements, which of course they were. She hadn't become a member of the Women's Association and this was enough of a transgression. But as a transplant, and a sort of perpetual stranger, she was still permitted a few eccentricities.

Before she had moved, Kris had said, "Why the hell Gull Harbor? You're not going to like it. Within a month you'll be fed up with all of the busybodies trying to figure out what dark secrets you're escaping from in Chicago, in part because that's the place they're trying to escape *to*. Goodbye Wrigley Field, hello church picnic. You didn't ever want to go to your company picnics and at least they served free beer."

She knew that Gull Harbor did not make good sense, except perhaps as the fulfillment of a long-cherished dream. The problem with that kind of dream, as Kris saw it, was that it often disappointed if it came true. Lynne ignored him and moved ahead alone, but in a different way, moved backward into the arms of her adolescent self who still lay frying on the beach or mooning over a summer crush at a sticky table in J & L's ice cream and candy shop on Hubbard Street. Many of the stores from twenty years ago were still alive and slightly profitable, and for the first year she lived in Gull Harbor, she had sometimes found herself disoriented by her heavier body, by the older face reflected back to her by the shop windows. She had found a cottage close to downtown, not on the lake, those properties overpriced for vacation-home buyers, but close enough that she could often smell the lake's coldness in the winter and its tangy fecundity in the summer. No place she lived had ever been lovelier, this small house with its clean air—wind on some mornings, breezes on others, once in a while a gale, which others in town complained about but she loved, these lake gales that blew down from Canada, stirring up high waves that thrillingly harassed the moored fishing vessels and sailboats.

When the waitress delivered the chipped coffee cup to Connie, the older woman did not complain. Lynne suspected she hadn't noticed. She was still grumbling about the two dressing-room offenders, Mike Watson and Lucas Kaiser, who had been taken away in handcuffs by store security, but no one had bothered to press charges after the police had taken them into custody. The boys had been let go, and undoubtedly gone on to become the heroes of their freshmen class.

It was after the coffee and lemon tart that one of the younger WAMs, Jill Holmes, started crying. Most of the other twenty-one pairs of eyes at the luncheon, along with Lynne's and her two waitresses', stared at her in dismay before many of them looked away. "I'm sorry," Jill sniffled. "I had to put Patsy to sleep this morning and it's hitting me now that when I get home, she won't be there in the entryway wagging her tail, hoping that it's time for me to feed her. Don was against us doing it, but the poor girl was suffering so much. Dr. Pfeffer said it would be best for her, even if it was very hard for us."

Most of the WAMs made sympathetic noises and Marietta got up to give her a hug. Lynne refilled her coffee cup and gave her a sad smile. "I'm so sorry," she said. "It's never easy to lose a pet."

"I'm sorry for you too, Jill," said Connie.

Jill tried to smile. "I guess it's nothing like what you and Brett have had to go through. I'm probably overreacting."

A pained hush crept over the room and Jill looked even more stricken. Connie's face froze and she nodded but said nothing. Jill opened her mouth but closed it again. A meager, tinkling chatter started up while Jill miserably picked up her coffee cup and took a sip, her eyes on the table. Connie seemed to be blinking very deliberately when Lynne cleared away her dessert plate. She glanced up at Lynne and said too loudly, "Maybe we should try coloring your hair the next time you come in. I've been using some new dyes that can really liven things up."

Lynne managed to keep from bristling. "Thanks, but I actually don't mind my natural color."

"Sooner or later you'll want to cover up the gray."

". . . I don't really think it's that bad yet."

"You'd be surprised what a good dye job can do."

"Don't listen to a word she says, Lynne," said Teresa Hilt. "She's used that same line on all of us. Your hair looks very nice. Don't start dyeing it yet. Once you do, you'll never be able to stop."

Teresa Hilt was the Gull Harbor Elementary school principal; she was close to sixty, already a widow, and the mother of two children who had both gone to New York City for college and stayed there. She came to most of the luncheons; she liked to take in all of the gossip, but rarely contributed any—by design, Lynne thought. Teresa had been the first person to welcome and introduce her in town; she had invited her to a Mardi Gras party and there she had met the first doctor who had hired her to do his office payroll. Teresa was a do-gooder, but not insufferable. Lynne liked her and for a while had thought they would become better friends than they so far had. But Teresa was busy, and so was she.

"I might even let it all go gray if that's what's supposed to happen," said Lynne.

"Good for you," said Teresa. "All of those dye chemicals make me nervous, but I'm too vain not to do it." She smiled at the hairdresser. "Lucky for you."

"If I can't exploit people's insecurities," said Connie, "how am I supposed to stay in business?"

"I don't know if Lynne is particularly insecure. Not about her hair, anyway."

"Not enough, in any case," said Connie. "But I'll win her over eventually."

"If that's what you want to call it," said Teresa dryly.

On their way out of the museum, Jill Holmes stopped Connie and apologized. Lynne was standing by the heavy wooden door that opened onto the parking lot, saying good-bye to the WAMs. The air smelled sweet from an easterly lake breeze and gulls circled the nearby streetlights, their cries almost unbearably piercing.

"I hope I didn't offend you," said Jill, smiling uncertainly. "I'm not myself today."

Connie looked at her for a long second before answering. "I know that." She turned and walked out to her car, leaving Jill to stare at her back until she decided to hurry after Connie and stop her again.

Lynne didn't hear what was said this time, but it was over very fast and then Jill was crying and Connie was driving out of the parking lot, her face showing nothing. Jill wiped her cheeks and got into her own car and left in a hurry, forgetting to signal as she turned right out of the lot onto Cook Street. A few other WAMs had seen the exchange but no one commented. They would do it later, of course, over the phone. Connie was not a villain but she was not liked unreservedly, whereas Jill Holmes seemed to be. There was no doubt, however, which woman had more clout with the WAMs and the town in general. A woman with a pair of scissors and a dead son could not easily be pilloried.

After work, after she had made dinner and drunk half a bottle of wine with her broiled piece of lake trout, Lynne dialed Jill's number. She had done this only once before, to accept an invitation to her daughter's high school graduation party, to which dozens of other people had been invited.

Jill's husband answered the phone and Lynne almost hung up when she heard his voice. She had no real idea what she was doing. Still, it had seemed necessary to call. She had always thought that small towns needed strangers, even if it was difficult to get anyone to admit this. Kris had been right about one thing—the Gull Harbor natives had been very surprised that she had left Chicago, but there was a schizophrenia active in their opinions—Chicago was superior, but so was the Harbor.

"Jill," said Lynne. "I hope I'm not disturbing you and Don. I just wanted to see how you were doing. I was so sorry to hear about your dog. I've been through that myself."

"You're so sweet to call. I'm doing better now, thanks. I probably shouldn't have gone to the luncheon, but I had already paid for it so it seemed best to go. What a wet blanket I was." She laughed nervously.

"No, you weren't. Not at all."

"No, I'm sure that I was."

Lynne tried to reassure her a second time and then couldn't think of anything more to say. There was no way to bring up Connie without forcing it. She could have invited Jill out for tea or brunch at Burton's Café, a mediocre, WAM-sanctioned restaurant, but she didn't know if Jill would want to go, and she also didn't know if she wanted to go either. Her three real friends in town were not WAMs; one was a high school history teacher, another a vegetarian chef who worked in Chicago four days each week, the third the program coordinator at the museum. Only the high school teacher wasn't a transplant.

Instead, it was Jill who made the invitation. "I've been meaning to call you ever since Stephanie's party. So many months ago now! I'm thinking of going to that new outlet mall near Benton Heights on Saturday. Would you like to join me?"

Without hesitating, Lynne said yes, and for the rest of the night she felt weirdly exhilarated. Perhaps she hated Connie. She hadn't thought so before now. It seemed that she would finally have to switch hair stylists. It also seemed that she was tired of looking the other way when certain people treated others poorly. And maybe she wanted a mister; maybe she wanted to be Brenda Wright? But without the muck of adultery to wade through. Lynne had not dated anyone in Gull Harbor during the fifteen months she had lived there. Kris had come to see her a few months after she had moved; they had slept together, which had been a mistake because he hadn't wanted to go back to Chicago without her. Their divorce had come through three months later and she hadn't seen him again after this, but they still called each other once in a while. She felt guilty for hurting him and thought that she might always feel guilty. She had preferred, before now, not to have to worry about a new man—one who might not want her enough or else want her to be someone different. A few of the WAMs had tried to set her up on blind dates, but she had turned them down, saying she needed more time before dating again. They had never been divorced, but they had pretended to understand. Before her separation from Kris, she had never lived alone. She found that she loved it.

On Saturday, Jill came by to pick her up at 9:30. Jill was wearing a pink short-sleeved blouse and a knee-length khaki skirt, her dark red hair twisted into a messy bun. She was very pretty, with her olive skin and long lashes. Lynne had on a pair of jeans and a sleeveless black turtleneck and felt underdressed, but she preferred jeans to anything else and could never wear them when working at the historical society. "You look nice," said Jill.

Lynne smiled. "You look even nicer."

"I usually overdo it, don't I. I don't know why I feel like I have to dress up to go shopping. I guess it's so that the salespeople will treat me with more respect."

"They also won't think you're going to steal anything, so it's easier to get away with it when you do."

Jill blinked, half-smiling.

"I'm just kidding," she said, feeling her face turn warm.

"Oh, of course! I'm a little dopey sometimes. Sorry."

"No need to apologize. My jokes aren't very funny."

Her face even warmer now, Lynne looked down at her hands and noticed that her nails needed to be filed. She didn't get regular manicures and never had. She had no idea what to say to Jill who she was pretty sure felt as painfully self-conscious as she did. After several long seconds, Jill glanced over and asked if she wanted her to change the radio station. "There's so little new music that I like," she said. "It all sounds pretty boring or just plain awful. Have you ever played an instrument?"

"The piano, a long time ago," said Lynne. "My parents got tired of me tormenting them with it when I was thirteen and let me quit."

"I used to play the clarinet and once thought that I'd play with an orchestra, but in college I figured out how much time you actually had to spend practicing if you wanted to be any good. You also had to have a lot of confidence, but I suppose that's true about any job worth doing."

"I'm not sure how to get confidence if you don't already have it though."

"You seem confident to me."

Lynne snorted. "My work isn't very hard."

"I don't mean about your work. You moved to a place where you didn't know a soul." Jill spoke emphatically, but her eyes stayed on the road. "I would never have been able to do that, if I'd even have thought of it."

"It can be much harder to stay where you are sometimes."

She shook her head. "I don't know about that. At least people would know you. There'd probably still be a few you could trust."

"In theory, I suppose."

Rain clouds were forming in the east when they got to the mall where they almost immediately began to spend money. With an embarrassed look, Jill told Lynne that she loved stuffed bears and took her into a toy-store outlet where she bought four bears of varying sizes. "I have no idea what I'll do with them," she said. "But they're so cute, don't you think?"

Lynne smiled. "They're adorable." The bears were very cute, each with button eyes, soft brown fur, and one in a pink bonnet and apron, but next to useless for a grown woman with no grandbabies or little kids of her own.

"My husband will think I'm nuts. But he's been pretty indulgent this week because of poor Patsy."

In the next store, they ransacked a clearance table of cashmere sweaters, and Lynne felt loose and happy, bargains often causing her to feel elated—an addict's behavior, Kris used to gripe. "What happened with Connie on Monday?" she asked, her eyes on the mound of sweaters. "I really didn't think you'd said anything offensive."

Jill froze, a mauve V-neck in one hand. "Monday? Do you mean at the luncheon?"

Lynne looked up. "Yes, but afterward, in the parking lot. You looked upset when you left. I was worried about you." She didn't think she was prying, not precisely. This was concern—of course it was, a desire to put a nice person at ease.

Jill shook her head. "I goofed up. Connie doesn't like to talk about her son and I shouldn't have said anything but it slipped out."

"You didn't do it on purpose. I think everyone knew that."

"Connie's been through so much and I know not to take what she says too personally. She blows up and then it's over and everything goes back to normal."

Lynne looked at her but said nothing.

"Seriously," said Jill. "Don't worry about me. I'd forgotten all about it."

"That's good," said Lynne, not believing her. "You're very kind not to have held whatever she said to you against her."

"It was nothing. Really. I can barely even remember it."

Lynne could tell that she was blowing this. Jill wouldn't meet her eyes as she folded the mauve V-neck and put it back on the table before walking over to a table heaped with scarves and belts. It had started to rain in fat, clamorous drops. Jill's bag of bears hung at her side, two sets of furry ears protruding from the top. The spectacle of her would-be friend's girlishness made Lynne feel worse. She was an idiot, a pathetic blunderer, to have brought up the scene at the luncheon. Connie might actually be unassailable—someone who would never leave Gull Harbor, and others knew this and arranged their opinions of her accordingly. Likewise, she was feared and pitied—a strange, vertiginous mix of feelings that no one else Lynne knew inspired.

When the rain lost its loud vigor, Jill suggested they go home. "If we stay, I'll just spend more money," she said, half apologetic. "Unless there's something you need that you haven't found yet?"

Lynne shook her head. "I've already found too much stuff I need."

"But it's been fun, hasn't it?" Jill smiled and brushed hair from her eyes. "We'll have to come again when we have something specific to shop for."

"That'd be nice," said Lynne, knowing she didn't sound convincing.

On the ride home, their conversation was forcibly innocuous. Would Jill and Don get a new dog? Would Lynne like to take on more accounting business, even if this was the full-time work she had happily left behind in Chicago? But just before Jill dropped her off, she gave Lynne an earnest look and said, "We all wonder if you're lonely. Don't you want to marry again or at least have a boyfriend?"

We all wonder . . . Jill would never have said *I wonder.* She was a mere functionary, Lynne could see, a small limb of a powerful body. What exactly had she expected? More importantly, what did she want from the WAMs? To be left alone but also regularly sought out, to be a member without actually *being* a member? She certainly couldn't have both.

"I don't know if I ever want to get married again," she said. "But at some point I think a boyfriend would be nice."

"You might change your mind about the husband. If you meet the right man."

"My ex-husband Kris might have been the right man. Maybe I'm not the right woman."

"I doubt that's the case."

She laughed. "Maybe I like women."

Jill faltered. "Oh? Oh," she said.

"I don't," said Lynne. "Another stupid joke. I like men, always have."

Why this embarrassing need to keep explaining herself? Jill wasn't dumb, but there did seem to be something willfully obtuse about her. For all of her niceness and her former clarinet-playing intelligence, she appeared, unfortunately, a bit dense. But this denseness might also have been a charade, something to keep her out of lasting trouble.

"I like men too," said Jill. "Lucky for Don."

They turned onto Lynne's street, and she wished she were already inside her house, sitting next to the open windows in the kitchen, the gulls' plaintive cries and the lake wind always comforting. "Thanks for inviting me," she said when Jill had pulled into the driveway. "It was nice to get away for a few hours."

"We'll have to do it again," said Jill.

"I hope so." She hesitated. "I'm sorry again about Patsy."

A tremor passed over Jill's face, but she only nodded. "Thanks, Lynne. We're doing a lot better than we were on Monday. I'll see you at the next luncheon if not before then."

"Yes, see you soon." She gathered her bags and left the car, making sure not to slam the door.

Jill waited for her to unlock the front door before pulling away. Lynne turned and waved but Jill was looking down, possibly fumbling in her purse for her phone. Once inside, Lynne dropped her shopping bags in the tiny mudroom off the foyer and went straight to the kitchen for a bag of cookies she had bought the day before. She ate five in brisk succession and fought the urge to call Kris who not long ago had started dating a woman whom she could see him marrying. But what would she have said to him—I went shopping and discovered that I've become a busybody? At best, he would have laughed and said, "I warned you, didn't I? For once in your life, you'd think you would have seen it coming." At worst, he would have told her to stop calling him, though she doubted he would mean it.

It didn't seem likely that she had made Jill into an enemy. Neither did it seem likely that Jill would say anything to Connie about her attempt to connive information about the parking lot scene. But who knew if Jill would tell someone else, and then Connie would know for certain that the short-banged, probable atheist from Chicago really wasn't to be trusted. What she would do with this information, however, could not be predicted. Connie was a businesswoman, after all, and Lynne her customer. Perhaps all she wanted was to be right. As far as Lynne could tell, this was something that everyone wanted.

She didn't think she would change hair salons right away. She was too tired to think about it. Somehow, she had permitted everyone in Gull Harbor to become a part of her life. They were all in her house, living with her. It was peculiar—at once exhilarating and distressing—but she could not see herself ever moving away.

A Million Dollars

For one, I am not as dumb as some people seem to think I am. He should know that only morons would ever fall for that old line—"Have I seen you somewhere before? Because you look like a model. You have to let me take your picture." That one ranks right up there with "If you start selling these vacuum cleaners, you'll soon be so rich you'll only have to work three weeks a year," or "This car's got a lot of miles on it, but it's still in mint condition." Whatever. The guy might be an idiot, but I'm not. Some people think that if you haven't gone to college, you're just sitting around waiting for someone to come over and mess with your weak little mind. It's true that after high school, instead of going downstate to the big-time university in the middle of cow and corn paradise, I moved only four miles from my parents' depressing house where they live their depressing lives with my little sister Penny, and got a job as a waitress at the Spaghetti Kitchen, but that doesn't mean I'm dumb.

This guy who said he wanted to take my picture wasn't even at one of my tables when he started to ogle me with his beady freak's eyes. I was serving this family of six—two crabby, eye-rolling parents, one crapped-on grandma and three loudmouth kids all under ten, when Mr. Model-maker glued his eyes to my boobs and said, "Hey! Sorry to bother you, but do I know you from somewhere? You look soooo familiar. Are you in the latest issue of *Glamour?*"

"As if!" I wanted to yell. "As if I'd be working here if I were some high-class model. Are you down to your last brain cell?" But instead I kind of laughed and said, "No, no, I'm just a waitress." Shit. *Just* a waitress. I have to stop saying things like that because people can tell when you're inse-cure. You might as well be wearing a sign that says *Kick me hard.* I have plans, as I suppose everyone says, whether they mean it or not. But I do mean it. I'm going to go to the community college in Newton starting in the summer to get a degree in hotel and restaurant management. It's only a two-year program, but some people who made a lot of money and had a lot of power didn't go to college. Some people, like Thomas Jefferson and his pals, wrote the Constitution and created this country but not all of them knew how to do calculus or speak Spanish or would even think to file away the difference between a polar molecule and a covalent bond in their big, wig-wearing heads.

The guy with the beady eyes kept it up for a long time. Whenever I'd hustle by his table with my tray full of ravioli or cheesy breadsticks or our twenty-four ounce glasses of demon-child-spawning Coke, Mr. Mod-elmaker would smile at me and say in a slithery voice that I was beautiful. I liked this and didn't like this. The freak wasn't ugly, but he was slimy. I could see that with his shirt open down to the third button and his silver chain with its weird-looking transparent rock, he had to be the kind of guy who spends a lot of time looking in the mirror before he leaves what-ever dingy apartment he lives in—unless he lives with his parents, which is entirely possible. I'd bet a hundred bucks that he's also the type of guy who would see if he could get you into bed on the very first date. On top of that, he'd probably get all shitty about wearing a condom. I knew it just by looking at him.

I thought about telling Paulie to come out of the kitchen and put his arm around me and show the necklace guy that I'm already taken but he would never do it, not in a million years. He and I have something going on that's supposed to be under the radar because he has a public girlfriend who isn't me. I'm his private one, I suppose, even though I don't think he or any other guy, no matter how handsome or rich and famous, needs two girlfriends, especially if one of the girlfriends goes around telling everyone that they are engaged. But no date's been set. No ring's been offered. Therefore, they are most definitely not engaged. But Stacie is a nutjob who thinks that every guy on the planet wants to boff her. Yeah, and every guy on the planet is so nice that the prisons are about to go out of business.

Finally, about two hours after he got to the restaurant, the necklace guy left. He gave me his card and told me to call him if I wanted to pose for him. He's a professional, he said, very classy. No strings and there'd be no sitting fee. He could help me get a portfolio together and send it to the people at the big modeling agencies in New York City and I'd have it made in no time. He'd done it for other knockouts before, out of the goodness of his heart. Did I know who Melanie Sphinx was? No? Well, I sure would soon.

On his card with its wedding-invitation script, it says his name is Linus Shrechter. Linus? I'm telling you, there's no way in hell that's his real name. If it were, I'm sure he would have changed it by now. So I have to wonder why on earth he'd pick the name of a nerdy Peanuts character for his fake name. He must want to seem like he's a harmless dope. What girl would ever think a guy named Linus would lure her to his so-called photographer's studio to rape her before dismembering her and burying her in his creepy basement? I should have given the card right back to him, but I didn't. No matter if he's a serial killer, I didn't want to hurt his feelings, I guess. I'm just not mean enough to do something like that. But give me another year at the Spaghetti Kitchen and I'll probably be as mean as anyone. Being nice to every single person who comes through the door so you can make your measly tips is really starting to get to me. Dad's favorite complaint is, "Most people's default mode is full-throttle fuck-youhood." But he's down on everyone right now because he was laid off from the paper mill with half the town last year and can't find a new job that he thinks is worth his time. Anyway, I'm realizing that he's probably right about the fuck-you-ness of other people, even though for a long while I thought that everyone would be nice to each other if they weren't given a reason not to be. What a crock that turned out to be.

When my shift ended and I finally got all of the cheapskates hogging my booths to pay up and clear out, I went into the kitchen to see if

Paulie would take me home and maybe stay for an hour. Paulie is not my first, but he is the best. I didn't know this until a few weeks after we met though. Unlike some of the skanks I used to know in high school, I don't give it up the second a guy asks if I want to see the new stereo in his car. Paulie's my fourth, which I haven't told him. But the other three were boyfriends, not smooth-talking scuzzballs I met at a party and let bang me in the back room of someone's parents' cruddy house. Paulie's the first guy I've been with who can actually locate the On switch on a girl's body without having to be shown. He finds it every time and doesn't get why other guys have a hard time. "What more do they need? Flashing lights?" He pretends it's no big deal but he's very proud of his skills, and himself in general. He kind of brags a lot, which is why when my sister met him after he and I started hanging out a few months ago, she didn't like him. "He looks like a rooster with that weird hair," she said. "And why did he have to do that thing with his crotch? Couldn't he have gone to the bathroom and done it in there instead?" He had to do that thing with his crotch because he's pretty big and sometimes he gets out of alignment down there. When he walks, he says it sometimes gets in the way and it can get squished. But Penny just looked at me funny when I told her this and laughed. "Whatever!" she shrieked. "I've never heard of that happening to any guy before. Paulie just likes to grab his package in front of cute girls. Face it, Thea. He's a perv!"

He is not a perv. And Penny is a retard. Even if she's smart school-wise. But so am I. I had a B average all the way through to graduation which is why Mr. Walker, the government teacher who is also one of the guidance counselors, told me I should go to a four-year college and not waste one second working for a restaurant or shoe store or movie theater, unless I'm taking classes too. He told me that looks fade and boys who now seem so great and cool grow up to be disillusioned men who cheat on their wives or else are cheated on by their wives. I sort of laughed and told him I wasn't planning to get married any time soon. He cleared his throat and said, "Good. Good. It's not something that should ever be rushed into." He said he just sees the big picture and sometimes can't keep himself from describing it.

When I go back to the kitchen, Paulie is on the phone and holds up a finger for me to wait and so I stand off to the side of the swinging doors, and the other two cooks, George and Manny, see me and give me the naked, sleazy eye. Paulie probably tells them too much but I don't really know what can I do about this. They work fifty or sixty hours a week together and during the slow times, he says, what are they going to talk about other than sports and pussy (which is his word, not mine)?

I'm sure he's on the phone with Stacie, the dumbest, skankiest girl in the state. It's a few minutes after eleven and most of the servers are doing their side work because everyone's tables have left except for two old slowpokes in the smoking section who aren't mine, thank God. I take a bread roll from the big basket near Manny, and he slaps my hand and laughs. "You'll get fat," he says.

I scowl at him. "I just busted my butt for six hours. I think I can eat one roll."

"I just busted my butt for six hours," he mimics. "It don't look busted to me, sweetheart."

"You're nasty," I say, tearing into the roll. I'm skinny, too skinny, according to Paulie, so I know Manny's just trying to get my goat. George snickers and wiggles his eyebrows at Manny and me. Paulie finally gets off the damn phone and comes over and puts his arm around my waist. I whisper that I want him to come home with me, but he shakes his head. "Can't tonight. Stacie wants to go out. We're going over to Rick's."

Rick's is the one bar in town where people can smoke pot in the back room. Rick's a pothead and his brother's the police chief and Rick could probably get away with running a whorehouse in the back room if he wanted to. I hate it when Paulie talks about Stacie and what he's going to do with her or what he's done with her or what she wants him to do, even when he's making fun of her. Why do you stay with her? I sometimes ask and his answer is always lame, something like "because she'd kill herself right now if I broke up with her," or "because her dad cheated on her mom," or "I'm going to dump her as soon as our lease expires," but it didn't expire because he says she went behind his back and forged his signature and renewed it.

In the parking lot, before Paulie gets into his car and I get into mine, I say, "A guy came in tonight who asked to take my picture. He said he's a photographer and could set me up with an agency in New York."

He pauses for a second, looks me up and down and says, "You should have him do it."

I stare at him. It's like he's just told me he's Satan or something. "I should?"

He nods. "You're hot. Why not? Maybe he's legit and could help you make a lot of money. Who knows?"

"What if he's a psychopath?"

"Bring Teresa or Penny or both of them with you."

"Why don't you come with me?"

"I would, but with work and Stacie, you know it's hard. Maybe you could ask your dad."

Yeah, and maybe I could ask Rick's brother, the chief of police. I'm so mad at Paulie that I get into my car without kissing him goodbye and I don't look at him one last time when I pass him on my way out of the lot. Not like it would really matter. Besides a retarded girlfriend, Paulie has a sick mother and a long-gone dad, so he has too many women asking him for too many things. I know I should bail on him, but I can't do it. Not yet, if ever. For one, he's too damn good at finding the On button. For two, and this is probably even more important, I keep having these really vivid dreams about him, and in them, we're living together in a big house and have two little boys. I know it's all coming, but I don't know how long it's going to take to get here.

I don't want to call the skeezy necklace guy Linus Schrecter. I know he's bad news like the guy in the movie who always says to his nicer friend, "Just try it this one time. No way will you get addicted." I haven't ever thought about being a model, at least not seriously. You've got to have a lot of money to get the right kind of pictures taken. Plus, I'm only 5'7" and I think you have to be at least 5'9" for anyone to really look at you in those fancy New York agencies. I don't have the cheekbones either. Mine don't stick out like they're waiting for snowflakes to land on them and complete the perfect picture of beautiful girly goodness.

But guess what, I do call Linus Schrecter. I do it because after five days, Paulie hasn't said one word about me putting myself in the hands of a possible rapist/serial killer who probably thinks he's going to get me out of my clothes and make me do sick things with dildos and whatnot. Paulie doesn't say squat about the necklace guy or coming over to my place after work or taking me down to Wisconsin Dells like he said he would last month for my nineteenth birthday which is only a few weeks away. Paulie can only bother himself to come over once during those five days about a half an hour before he's supposed to be at work. He wants me to get all lovey-dovey on him for twenty minutes. Twenty lousy minutes and he thinks I should be grateful. He thinks I should hang his picture all over my walls and write songs about him and dance around with tassels on my nipples I'm so damn grateful he's coming over to spend twenty friggin' minutes getting his rocks off before he goes to work and tells George and Manny just how hot his shit is.

Teresa, my best friend, who is almost engaged to a guy named Magnus who is a complete tool, thinks I'm an idiot for bothering with Paulie. "So what if he can make you come in three minutes! That doesn't mean he's the right guy for you. If he's cheating on Stacie, what's going to stop him from cheating on you?" Penny has said pretty much the same thing. She's sixteen and has her own tool-ish boyfriend and thinks she knows everything. But the difference between Stacie and me is, Paulie actually likes me as a person and only puts up with her. It might sound like I'm a total idiot, but I'm not. He doesn't pull the twenty-minute crap that often. Some weeks he does come over after work and once he even stayed the night when Stacie was in Milwaukee visiting her grandmother. She called him about five hundred times, but he was still in my bed the whole night.

Linus Schrecter doesn't answer his phone. I get voicemail with a generic greeting but I go ahead and say who I am. I also say that I want to see some of his work before I commit to anything. I'm not going over to his place either—he can come to the restaurant and show me some of his stuff there. I have to wonder what Paulie will say about this. It's not like he has the right to be jealous but I wouldn't mind riling him up a little bit, seeing as how I spend half of my life these days getting riled up. But if everything went smoothly all of the time, how boring would that be? They don't make TV shows and movies about couples who are happy and never fight. They make TV shows and movies about couples who get separated by mean bosses and evil kings or weirdos and pervs in general but then somehow find a way to get back to each other and have great, window-rattling sex and cool apartments in New York and Los Angeles.

Linus Schrecter doesn't call me back that day or the next. I wonder what the hell his problem is, acting all hot and bothered when he met me and now doing squat about it when he has the chance. But maybe he was in a car wreck or got called to New York suddenly or his dog got run over by a bus and he's not himself right now. Yeah, right. And I'm Nicole Kidman.

Well, it turns out I'm just really impatient. It turns out that some people, for reasons they never explain, take their time. Which I almost never do, even if I should, at least according to my dad and Mr. Walker. My shift starts at five o'clock a few nights after I left Linus that message, which means I'll get a bunch of old people who leave a five percent tip and act like they're doing me a huge favor, some of them even handing me the dollar-fifty and saying I should save it for college. Do I have a piggy bank just for college money? Do they friggin' squeak when they walk they're so friggin' tight?

At five-forty-five, Linus Schrecter shows up with this big black folder under one arm and his hair slicked back and two weird crystal rocks on silver chains this time. He gets himself seated in my section and I feel my heart speed up a little when I see him there, a big shit-eating grin on his face, and his shirt open down to the third button again. He's wearing cologne, something that smells good, but it's a little too much. He's got chest hair too, which is something I like. I don't like his, not necessarily, but I do like Paulie's. "Hey, beautiful," says Linus. "I can't tell you how happy I am you called."

I feel my face get hot. "I'm not saying I'll pose for you."

"No worries. I understand. But I think you'll like what I can do." He opens the folder and starts to take out a few pictures but right then, I can't stick around. Greg the owner is here tonight, stalking the floor, making sure no one steals one grain of salt or wastes one second having a good time.

"You'll have to show me a little later. The boss is over there." I tilt my head to the right, keeping my voice down.

"You really shouldn't have to work at a place like this," says Linus. "You could be modeling within the month."

"I doubt that," I snort, trying not to roll my eyes. I ask for his drink order before returning to the table of four seniors who need their five-hundredth refill of coffee to go with their early bird specials of cheese lasagna and cups of minestrone, which always has "too much juice and not enough wholesome vegetables." Their bill will be $26.84, not a penny more. It's the same each Thursday night but they check every single item on it. I'm not down on old people but I really hate cheapskates. Before working here, I would never have believed there were so many of them out there. Linus is right—I shouldn't be working someplace like this, but leaving would mean that I would hardly get to see Paulie. And on good nights, I can make eighty bucks or more. Luckily, good nights usually out-number the bad nights.

When Greg goes down to the basement with one of the busboys to get more cans of tomato sauce, I run over to Linus and tell him to show me the pictures. He smiles that scary smile again but I'm getting better at looking past it. I can also see that he's not that young—maybe forty or even older, with wrinkles around his eyes and gray in his hair that I bet he dyes but hasn't lately. But his pictures, well, they are really good. Not like I really know what I'm talking about, but they look as good as anything I've seen in *Cosmo* or *Vogue*. The girls are so pretty, prettier than I am, but maybe it's the make-up or the lighting. He's even got some of a couple of guys in there—really cute guys with muscular bodies. They don't have little pots like Paulie does, from too much spaghetti and the beer that he and Stacie drink. I've never seen guys like these models. Not in the flesh. I wouldn't know what to say to them if I ever did. "Hi. What's your name? I'm Thea," just wouldn't cut it, I bet.

"They're nice," is all I say.

"You think about it," he says. "I'm not trying to scam you. I could help you get out of here, and out of Sill's Creek."

"What are you doing here if it's so terrible?"

"I live in Chicago, but I had to come up for a little while to help my mom get the house ready for sale before we move her into assisted living. My dad died last year, and it's time for Mom and me to face facts."

"I'm sorry about your dad."

"Thanks."

I'm not sure if I should believe him though and he knows it.

He's kind of smiling, sort of nervous. "What?"

"Why do you have a business card with a local address if you're only in town for a little while?"

"I make my cards on the computer. They're nothing special." He shakes his head. "Damn, you're a tough one. If you don't want to be a model, maybe you could be a detective."

"I should get back to work. My boss will be back up here any second."

"Seriously, Thea, give me a shot. You won't be disappointed."

He leaves me a ten-dollar tip on a fifteen-dollar check. If he's for real, what he's been telling me is that I'm actually beautiful. That I could be famous too. That I could make a million dollars, maybe millions and millions of dollars. Which means I could give my parents a lot of money and my dad wouldn't have to keep looking for a job, one better than a pizza deliveryman or a newspaper guy, and my mom wouldn't have to work in the principal's office at Thompson Elementary if she didn't want to. I could pay for my college and Penny's college and meet men like the models in Linus's folder and make one of them fall in love with me if I decide I don't want to be with Paulie anymore, though he would probably dump Stacie if I became famous. I'm not used to thinking of myself as beautiful. The word makes my stomach feel strange, as if I'm about to plunge down the big hill behind the high school on my bike. Since he told me eight days ago that he wants to take my picture, I have been staring at my face in the mirror so much that it no longer looks like my face. I'm so bored with it too. There's nothing there that surprises me like the prettiest people in the magazines always do.

Because Teresa would ask Magnus if she could go with me and he would say no, Penny's the one I ask to go to Linus's. She says she'll do it, but I can tell she's jealous.

"He just wants to have sex with you, Thea. You're pretty but you're not Heidi Klum."

"I know that, but models don't go around looking like models all the time. Most of it's probably lighting and make-up."

Penny rolls her eyes. "Whatever you say."

"If you're going to be a pain, don't come. I don't want you screwing this up for me."

"Maybe he'll want to take my picture too."

"Don't you dare ask him. If he wants to, he'll tell you."

"I'm not going to say anything," she says, acting as if I'm a jerk to even mention it. "I'm not a total egomaniac."

Linus's address is on Mill Street; it's one of the old row houses that used to be filled with kids and dogs and parents who worked for the paper mill that closed down because the guys in charge stole all of its money and the place went into huge debt. Now half the houses on Mill are empty, with overgrown lawns and cracked driveways. The banks foreclosed on them and the people who used to live there moved to skid row or hell in a handbasket or to the lame trailer park over by the fairgrounds where burnouts do donuts in the dust with their souped-up cars and think they're so cool.

Linus's house isn't so bad, but there's no way it's going to sell fast, even with the nice flowers and big apple tree in the front yard. There's a new Ford Focus in the driveway with an Illinois plate. Not really the kind of car I'd expect him to drive but I'm glad to see that he's not lying about living in Chicago. Maybe I was wrong about him—maybe he's not a scuzz-ball. Maybe he really is a nice guy and does want to help me out, a total stranger to him but supposedly a beautiful one. These things can happen. At least in the movies they do, and movies are supposed to reflect real life, even if not many of the ones I've ever seen actually do.

When we're getting out of the car, I start wondering if his mom is home. It just seems weird, having an old woman there who will see me in my bikini. I brought two swimsuits with me, a couple of short skirts and tank tops, my prom dress from last year, and four other dresses, most of them short. It's what Linus said to bring. He didn't say anything about lingerie, but I brought a matching bra and panty set that I got for Paulie who maybe would be furious if he knew I were showing it off to another guy, even if I'm not going to have sex with him. Linus told me to put my hair up, and said it'd be best if I went to a salon to have them style it up and off my face. It cost me twenty bucks, but I did it.

Linus answers the door and he's wearing one of his dumb crystal necklaces again but his shirt is only open to the second button and he didn't overdo it with the cologne. He smiles at Penny and me and looks a lot less slimy than he did at the Spaghetti Kitchen. I can tell Penny is surprised, and I'm glad. I love her but she's a know-it-all and if she weren't a pretty decent person, I don't know if I'd like her that much, sister or no sister.

The front room has two armchairs and a sofa and a bunch of family pictures on the wall. It's a clean place and smells like baking apples, though it could be one of those Plug-ins that always fake me out. His mom isn't anywhere that I can see, but somewhere in the house, there's a radio on, tuned to some jabber-jaw station, no music, the kind Paulie and my dad both like but I don't at all.

After I introduce Penny and Linus gets us each a can of 7-Up from the kitchen, he takes us down some stairs into a basement where three tall, bright lamps are, and there's a big sheet with a swirly maroon design and a second sky blue sheet tacked to the walls. Linus grabs a fancy camera and takes my picture. "A candid," he says. "I want a few of you when you're not posing." I nod and smile and look over at Penny who's sitting on a stool by the stairs. He snaps another one. I feel very shy. The only pictures I've ever really posed for were yearbook pictures, which always made me look like I was one brain cell away from being retarded.

"How do you make any money doing this?" asks Miss Know-it-all. I shoot her a furious look but she ignores it.

Linus doesn't seem to mind. "I do commercial photography for a few ad agencies in Chicago. I do some portraits too, but I'm trying to get more assignments for magazines and hope to do more fashion photography, but it's very hard to break into."

"You actually think my sister could be a model," she says, her voice kind of hard.

"Yes, but first we need to touch up her make-up." He glances at me. "You brought it with you, didn't you?"

I did, all of it too—a bulging bag full of more make-up than any girl in her right mind would ever need, but Linus doesn't bat an eye. After I've put on all the mascara and eyeliner and blush he wants, I look like a tramp, but he says if I don't wear that much, I'll look washed out.

"Wow," says Penny. "Should I call Bozo to see if he wants to try your new look?"

I glare at her. "Should I call Jay Leno and tell him how funny you are?"

We start with one of the short dresses and then do a tank top and skirt before the bikini, and he clicks what must be about a hundred shots of each outfit. At first I feel like a total weirdo, having him stare at me so much and knowing Penny thinks I think I'm hot shit, but she's the only person I knew who would come with me for sure. I told Paulie we were coming too, in case something happened to Penny and me, but he didn't seem worried. "Get me some hot pictures," he said. "Something I can whack off to." I just stared at him for a long time before saying he was a pig. He made oinking noises and I wanted to kill him but instead acted like he wasn't there. If I do become famous, he's going to have a lot of kissing up to do. He's going to have to work on his gut too.

The whole shoot takes about three hours and when it's over, my face feels stiff from frowning and looking vampy and girl-next-doorish and bored and sincere and seductive and happy—all the instructions he gave me. I had to spend a lot of time staring past the lights that were cocked in my direction. He didn't ask me to put on the lingerie, maybe because Penny was there, and he talked nicely to me the whole time, as if he was a guidance counselor like Mr. Walker, telling me how great I can be. Sometimes he put his hands on my arms or back or face, but very polite, to help me get into a pose. I tried not to think about it too much, but I started to wonder if maybe I could be a model. Maybe I could model petites or do sales flyers for Kohl's or Penney's, just to get some experience before I took my best shots to New York and got a real assignment.

When I've packed up all of my things, he says he'll get in touch with me in a few days. He used a digital camera, so he'll have me back to look at the shots on his computer and then we can decide which ones to turn into prints. He says I did a great job and that he's very excited about the possibilities. He says maybe we'll do another session in a week or two if he thinks we need more shots. But then he does something that really ticks me off. It makes me wonder about what I was just doing on my first day off in nine days. What he does is, he gives Penny his card and tells her she should think about posing for him too. She blushes but then tries to act like it's no big deal, and maybe he isn't really serious, but he shouldn't have done it, not in front me.

Once we're in the car, she says, "I think you like him. I think you've got a crush on him. Look out Paulie."

"I don't have a crush on him and I don't think you should pose for him. You're too young."

"That's not true. Don't be so bitchy."

"You shouldn't swear."

"As if you never do, Miss Hypocrite."

"No offense, but he was probably just being nice to you."

Penny doesn't say anything. Then I start to feel even worse. "Do what you want to do," I say.

"You don't have to worry about it."

"If you do pose for him, I should go with you."

"I said, don't worry about it."

Then neither of us says anything for a while. She stares out the window and I glare at the road, wondering why I have to be so friggin' jealous of everyone. We're almost home before I say, "Thanks for going with me. It wasn't as bad as I thought it would be."

"He looks like he's as old as Dad. If you want to go out with him, just know you'll be going out with a guy who could have gone to school with Dad."

She could be right. Dad is forty-one. Linus looks like he's close. He has those wrinkles around his eyes and the gray hairs. "I'm not going to date him. I'm dating Paulie."

"If that's what you want to call it."

I look over at her, mad again, but she won't look at me. "You're being such an ass today, Penny."

"Like you aren't?" She's mad too but I know she's not going to freak out on me. She's too hurt that I don't think she could be a model. Maybe she could be, but I want to do it first. I want to be famous before her because I'm older and I think I deserve it. There might be people out there nicer than I am, but I'm not ever really mean, at least not that often. Some would say I'm being mean to Stacie, but it's Paulie's fault more than it's mine. I love him. I can't help that I feel that way. It doesn't seem wrong, and if he doesn't love her, she should let him go. There's nothing more pathetic than begging or tricking a guy into staying with you. If it weren't me, he'd probably be cheating on her with someone else. I know that's not exactly a good excuse, but it's not like she's my friend and I'm doing this behind her back. He's the one who should feel guilty.

I drop Penny at the house and don't go inside, even if I know Dad would like to see me. I just can't do it. Not today. Seeing him always makes me feel like garbage. He and Mom aren't getting along very well and I love him but Mom does have a point—even if he can't find a great job, he could still work part-time at the grocery store stocking shelves or being a cashier, or else waiting tables like I do. He says he's a skilled laborer, almost like an engineer because he was a machinist at the paper mill, but there aren't any jobs like his old one around here right now. He and Mom need money and he needs to get off his high horse, but I would never say this to him because he would get so mad I'd be afraid he'd yell so loud he'd burst my eardrums.

Linus doesn't call me after three days. I try calling him on the fourth day, but he doesn't answer. I leave a message and then another one the next day, and on the sixth day, I go over to his house. I'm by myself and I know this is stupid but I do it anyway.

His car isn't there, but I ring the doorbell. No answer. I ring it again. Then a third time. When I'm about to walk away, the door opens. It's his mom. She's a little stooped but not too weak-looking. She's wearing a pink cardigan and a pair of yellow slacks that are too big for her, and she looks at me like I'm trying to sell her something worthless. She stares, waiting for me to talk.

"Is Linus home?"

She shakes her head. "Nope, he's back in Chicago now."

My stomach gets kind of sick. "Is he coming back?"

"Probably in a week or two, but it could be longer."

"I was here last week with my sister. He took my picture, and he told me he'd have me over again to pick out the ones I want for my portfolio. Did he say anything to you about me?"

She sort of squints at me but doesn't look so suspicious anymore. "He's had a few young people over here for pictures. He's a hard worker."

My stomach feels even sicker. "I was hoping we could put a portfolio together this week."

"I don't know anything about that. I can tell him you stopped by when I talk to him next."

"Do you have a number for him in Chicago?"

"All he's got is that cell phone of his. He doesn't have a home phone."

"Did he put portfolios together for those other people?"

"I don't know. I don't think so."

After I apologize for bothering her, after I go home and cry and call in sick to work and eat half of the stuff in my refrigerator and get sick and puke it back up, I feel something weird like relief. As if it was never going to happen anyway and it's better that I find out now. But I don't know why he had to lie about all of it. I know he must only have been practicing for when he gets real models to pose for him, and I don't know why he couldn't have just said he wanted to take my picture because he needed to practice his technique. He didn't need to say all of that bullshit about recognizing me and thinking I was famous and in *Glamour,* and how he'd helped make Melanie Sphinx famous, whoever the hell that is. Nobody, that's who. She's just someone he made up for another nobody like me. Maybe the pictures turned out so bad he laughed when he saw them and thought to himself, "They'd have to shoot this chick from the neck down." I don't know what his stupid problem is, but it all just totally sucks.

Penny wants to know what's going on with the portfolio, and Paulie wants to know where his whacking-off pictures are and I tell them both that Linus lost them. That his computer crashed and he lost them. Penny knows I'm lying but doesn't say anything. Paulie doesn't know I'm lying because he's too dumb to know it.

I call Linus once more and this time, for some reason I will never understand, he picks up. I ask him why he didn't call me back. Why he left without helping me make a portfolio. He's at least nice enough to apologize. "Work's been so crazy, Thea," he says. "I haven't had time to call anyone. I'm sorry to leave you hanging. I should have told you earlier that if you want to get any of the photos printed, it's pretty expensive. I don't charge a sitting fee, but the prints themselves can cost about forty dollars a piece, and that's on the cheap side. If you want to do it, I have a good service I can send them too, but it's going to be a little while before I can get up there again. My mom's decided to wait on selling the house. We're going to try to rent it instead because the market's so bad. I can call you when I'm up there again. Sorry about this." He's kind of laughing like he's embarrassed. "Your shots were great though. You've got a chance. It's an extremely tough field to break into, but you can always try."

I can always try. Yes, I suppose I can. I can always try to avoid getting taken for a ride by some other crystal-necklace-wearing lowlife smooth-talker scuzzball. I can try to avoid wasting my time thinking that I am better or smarter or prettier or nicer than the next person and the next person and the next. I know that we are always supposed to try to be humble, that we are supposed to play the rotten hand we're dealt and make the best of it without complaining, but that's a load of crap if I've ever heard one. That's a total bullshit saying made up by a loser with a capital L. What I want is a real boyfriend, a real job, a real life in a real city that's got good movie theaters and coffee places on every corner and nice stores that you don't have to drive half an hour to get to before you find out they don't have what you want. Sill's Creek and Newton and Hillview where my parents and sister live are fine if all you want to do is watch crap TV every day and eat hamburgers and spaghetti and talk trash about people who eat tofu and sushi and buy three-dollar cups of organic coffee. It's because you can't afford those things. Or you're afraid of those things. Or you're afraid people like that won't like you. You're afraid of all of the traffic and fancy restaurants and people supposedly walking around with machine guns in their back pockets just waiting to pop you one. You're afraid and you're a stranger there, a hick in fact, and that's all there is to it.

Walled City

Wednesday is the day with the highest number of calls, the phone ringing as often as seventy-five times an hour, some of the calls going to voicemail because the operator cannot bear to put another irascible person on hold. Friday is the quietest day, the calls tapering off around one o'clock to only a few an hour, though there's a flurry right at five, most of them left to ring, the noise turning plaintive when previously it had seemed purposeful. This office is the clearinghouse, the repository for much that preoccupies the population of a once-thriving walled city, one where street musicians must apply for permits that never come, and neighborhood kickballers are required to pass first aid classes before launching projectiles at each other. Any behavior that creates even the mildest disturbance is generally frowned upon, few daring to leave the house without smoothing down unruly hairs and primly buttoning shirts and coats. Support hose, camisoles, sock garters, and girdles have made a furious comeback, the lingerie section of the department store in the main square cleared out an hour after a new shipment arrives, all of the hangers suspended in a graceless jumble on the racks, the floor supervisor unsure of whether to congratulate or chastise his salespeople. Most of the dogs have shrunk to the size of a dachshund—the retrievers, Labradors, Great Danes and huskies, once so popular, are now an affront, the sidewalks too small for two such dog walkers to pass politely by one another on an evening walk.

The office where the disgruntled file their complaints is hidden within a cavernous building near the southwestern portal of the city, its address known only to the mayor, her closest aide, and the operator charged with documenting the grievances; also, two janitors known for their discretion. There would be endless, snaking lines if the address got out, the streets nearby clogged with angry, harried citizens who would consider this mob scene yet another assault on their peace of mind—one of the inalienable rights so often discounted in favor of communal living, of the interpersonal commerce necessary to uphold a superior quality of life. There are so many rules, this being chief among the complaints, though also the fact that there is not yet a rule stipulating the number of plastic garbage bags, carefully sealed, one may place each morning in the sky-blue dumpsters adorning every street corner. A few people have been spotted tossing away as many as six hulking bags at one time, their faces carefully disguised by a shawl or a pair of dark glasses. None of the affronted, however, will approach these selfish individuals, for fear of speaking frankly in public to a stranger—this could be ruled defamation of character, a crime punishable by exile to an unprotected city where the majority of the population consists of other exiles, degenerate humans who think nothing of swimming in ill-fitting bathing suits at the crowded and filthy public beaches while letting their children scream deliriously and use their sand pails and shovels as makeshift drums.

The hotline, a legacy from the current mayor's predecessor, is nothing but a headache for all involved, but there is no logical way to dismantle it. The suggestion boxes in the public squares are already stuffed to bursting and the police force grievously overworked. Often the police are called upon to defuse a domestic situation that proves to be far from life-threatening, only an argument over the soundness of a microwave versus a conventional oven, because outdoor charcoal and gas grills, once the preferred cooking apparatuses, have been outlawed due to a few unrelated and costly conflagrations. The apologetic police officers must thus admonish families to be thankful for the resources still available to them.

After all, in the world outside their walls, anything goes, and the smoggy pollution from frequent diner grease fires is now a known carcinogen.

At a recent town meeting, one where the agenda is always planned painstakingly in advance, the most pressing concerns taken from the hotline and suggestion boxes, a prominent citizen spoke out of turn, offering the incendiary recommendation that a supervised Zone of Extraordinary Recreation be created, one where barbecuing, donut-frying and games of horseshoes once again be allowed, though of course only for a few hours on Friday nights, during the months of January, May and October, so as not to become a commonplace or an inducement to addiction. The suggestion was overruled, however, and the prominent citizen retreated into his home, squandering all of his considerable surplus hours of internet access within a two-day period, in part to research remote islands where people pledged allegiance to the sun alone.

The hotline operator has lately been inundated with complaints concerning the high school board's unaccountable privileging of scholars over athletes, the town's college scholarships awarded to the math and science prodigies this spring instead of to the basketball and football stars. What has happened to tradition? The rewards for those who achieve glory through a disciplined physical regimen, rather than those who are born knowing numbers can be multiplied and divided, made imaginary or confined to the lines of a triangle? Also, why are so many men stalling so long between haircuts while women have never before seemed more eager to chop off all of their hair in the manner of a reform-school boy?

The operator is aware, having come from a town outside of the wall, having also been trained in rudimentary psychology and crisis intervention, that the citizens of this town yearn for nothing more keenly than a catastrophe of Leviathan proportions. But none ever materializes—only paltry offenses that are inflated into examples of utmost depravity, in particular, a record store owner's attempt to burn down his own shop with the hope of collecting insurance money for his first edition Beatles records that no one has ever expressed any interest in because vinyl is considered hopelessly outdated, of interest solely to hippies and other detestable weirdos.

Also noticeable, and never discussed with anyone but the operator, is an alarming number of citizens' dissatisfaction with their sex lives. Because pornography merchants and psychotherapists have been outlawed, people find they have no one to turn to for relief, other than to their partners who mostly express mortification the moment sexual matters are alluded to. The population appears to have transmogrified into a collective of guilty masturbators, the birth rate in perilous decline as couples increasingly sleep in separate beds, sex awarded solely on special occasions—birthdays, anniversaries, after tree-planting ceremonies and the dedications of new office buildings.

The operator, a sagacious woman named Penny, a spinster sired by two itinerant teachers, and born beside the lawless banks of the Mississippi, has begun to suspect that the blind devotion to rule-making has succeeded in pilfering joy from every natural impulse, be it pure or lascivious, worldly or holy. In weekly conference with the mayor and her closest aide, the operator has confided her views, all three having agreed that upheaval and reform are necessary. This decision was reached after a particularly dispiriting week of complaints, the highlights of which were:

—infelicitous awakening at 1 a.m. when neighbor's car backfired twice, which led citizen to demand that all cars be parked in lots or stowed in garages by 11:30 every night without exception

—garments made from day-glo or garishly patterned fabrics, especially those worn by the obese and the aging, should be consigned to the trash heap

—rice should be served with school lunches in lieu of pasta and bread because wheat is a digestive adversary

—people who use walkers or canes crowding up sidewalks while others try to complete their early morning jogs; the elderly should only be allowed to take walks between 10 a.m. and 2 p.m. or else confine themselves to drainage ditches

—irritation over the paltry amount of sand in Prosperity Park's three sandboxes

—cats yowling while mating in alleyways at all hours

—young women parading around braless, inciting lust in weak-minded husbands and fiancés

—people conversing or laughing loudly while riding public transportation; all should be taught sign language in elementary school and required to use it whenever in public

—Morton Supermarket's chronic shortage of fudge pops during summer months

—anyone stung by a wasp or a bee should be awarded a hundred-dollar consolation gift for each sting suffered; this will keep people working in their gardens, devoted to the town's beautification initiatives

"Folly," mutters the mayor's aide, his eyes red from sleep-deprivation, the ceaseless litany of complaints he must address echoing through his head whenever he tries to sleep.

"I have to do something," says the mayor, her husband and two sons among those who most often file grievances, usually about their parking tickets and traffic violations.

"Impose a ban on all conversation, both public and private," offers Penny, half in jest, but the mayor and the aide turn to her, their interest earnest and smoldering.

"For how long?" asks the mayor.

"When?" asks the aide. "Immediately?"

"But will I lose my job?" asks Penny, hoping she doesn't appear too selfish.

The mayor shakes her head, but the aide looks skeptical, remembering the previous operator, one to whom a raise was promised, and a vacation, but was let go when she called in sick two days in a row not long before the raise was due to take effect. Promises, in this town, are the main currency, one constantly being devalued by its abundance.

Within three days, the mayor announces her decision to mandate an end to all conversation—no phone calls, no spoken greetings or friendly chats in public squares, in stores or at home. "This is a time of reflection," she declares, "a time of retreat from all of our petty concerns. Only I can break the silence, and I have not yet determined when this will be."

To set an example, she incarcerates her youngest son who cracks a joke in his school classroom when he hears that his mother, an often well-meaning woman but a true windbag, has banned all oral communication.

Penny does not lose her job, though her life, stripped of all of the gripes that once made it so vital if not also exhausting, seems little more than a molted skin. She has enough good sense, however, to recognize that she should allow peace to prevail, contemplation to feed her wit. After a grueling year and a half, she has been freed from the endless weekday clamor of telephones. All suddenly seems fair. She works crosswords and accidentally waters her plants until they swim in their clay pots. Even though no one is allowed to talk, to chatter, to babble, to complain, to mimic, to mutter, to mumble, to snap, to cry, to shout, to whimper, to wail, music is permitted, but only the kind played by professionals in sanctioned locations. In almost every house, a symphony gently pours forth from a CD player or a radio—no rock or rap or country or pop—only classical, and none of it by contemporary composers, whose music is considered the aural equivalent of sandpaper.

The town settles into a soporific state, an atmosphere of tranquility prevailing for the first time in more than a decade, a time when there was no hotline, no suggestion boxes; when kite-flying and hot air balloon rides were the most popular leisure activities, along with a carefully supervised boxing class at the now defunct YMCA.

Once all chatter stops, outrage over other people's inadequacies and selfishness moves below the surface and seems, for a while, to have disappeared entirely. No one honks at stoplights. People picnic on hillsides, no longer glaring at their neighbors' dogs and kids. The mayor does not know why she waited so long to make this decree. The aide also feels relief and sleeps for several hours at a time, his renewed energy making it nearly impossible for him not to talk.

But then, after five months of quiet and calm, most of the population has learned sign language and soon the grievances are again proliferating. Strangers begin to gesticulate angrily at each other on the bus, in the store, on the sidewalk, alarming grimaces on their faces as they flail wrathfully, some of them so angry that they end up locking their arms around the offenders, squeezing the air from their lungs. At first doctors aren't sure what to do when a suffocating victim arrives at the emergency room, the decree of silence still not lifted, and few of the doctors having had the time to learn sign language, having opted instead to begin writing legibly.

The mayor, however, so enamored now of the absence of argument and reprimand, is reluctant to lift the ban, despite the town's increasing casualties, realizing in a revealing moment of introspection that she does not care if her constituents crush each other to death, something she eventually communicates to Penny, by way of a typewritten letter, one that somehow falls into the hands of a prominent citizen, the resentful wife of a blind man who will never learn sign language.

Within a matter of hours, the mayor is ousted, her own family joining the mob of turncoats who thrust her out of the cramped northeastern portal, her legs and arms bleeding and scraped, her unpracticed voice too weak to call for help. She is soon picked up by a traveling salesman who believes her to be a mute, shouts nonsense at her and then drops her at a ramshackle hospital where her abrasions are treated with expired iodine and bandaged with discolored gauze. The ministering doctor and nurse, however, smile kindly at the devastated mayor and tell her jokes about golfers, one-legged prostitutes, and priests, the kind never heard in the walled city.

The home from which she has been exiled extends its brick walls into the clouds, the mayor watching the progress from a hut she builds in a grove near the borderlands, wondering, with burning malice, what has happened to Penny—the person (an outsider! she remembers) responsible for all of the calamity that has befallen her beloved, unreachable home. She does not know that Penny, still loyal, has left the city to find her, hoping to take the mayor traveling, to introduce her to her brother who is unmarried and miserable, though fairly wealthy. Two such people might be capable of overcoming any difficulty, of reclaiming the walled city and transforming it into a less contentious community. Yet, this could only be accomplished if they didn't henpeck each other too severely, seeing as how one has a tendency to mispronounce words and forget to brush her teeth, and the other sometimes stares in the mirror for half the morning, worrying about his moles. Penny is aware that great, far-sighted plans can be toppled by the merest twinge of spite, as happened when an exalted architect argued briefly but fatefully with a carpenter over the size and location of keyholes, the carpenter knowing his opinion to be unassailable though of course it wasn't heeded. He avenged himself by placing all of the building's two hundred and eight doorknobs and keyholes three inches from the top of the door, and on the morning when the city officials came to inspect the building, they hastily withdrew the architect from his next project for the city. The carpenter was never located, the architect ruined by rage and shame, becoming a drunkard, as Penny worries has also happened to the mayor who could never be trusted to disregard the decanters of brandy and rum in her city hall office.

Yet, when morosely drunk, the mayor was sometimes wise and had once said that people would not stop until every mystery had been buried or decimated, every kindness diminished to rumor, to myth. Penny had tried to argue with her, saying that not everyone was petty and cruel, but the mayor had stared at her and declared that she knew nothing. Any person who did not see her point of view was a hateful idiot, especially one who kept an aquarium of tiny frogs, pets so small that she couldn't see them without a magnifying glass, and had named her car Trixie, which was in fact a description of the mayor herself, but Penny was too generous and intelligent to argue with a grieving drunk.

CHRISTINE SNEED was raised in Green Bay, Wisconsin, and Libertyville, Illinois. She earned a bachelor's degree in French language and literature at Georgetown University and graduated from Indiana University's MFA creative writing program with a poetry concentration. She teaches creative writing and literature courses at DePaul University and currently resides in Evanston, Illinois. She has been awarded an Illinois Arts Council fellowship in poetry, has been nominated for five Pushcart Prizes, and has published more than thirty short stories since her first appeared in *The Laurel Review* in 1999. Her work has appeared or is forthcoming in *Best American Short Stories, Ploughshares, New England Review, The Southern Review, Meridian, Greensboro Review,* and a number of other journals.